THE TETHERING LIGHT

BOOK ONE - THE GUARDIAN'S THREAD

A NOVELLA

CARYS LLEWELYN

Copyright © 2025 Carys Llewelyn

All rights reserved.

No part of this publication may be reproduced, distributed, or transmitted in any form or by any means, including photocopying, recording, or other electronic or mechanical methods, without the prior written permission of the publisher, except in the case of brief quotations used in reviews or critical articles.

This is a work of fiction. Names, characters, places, and incidents are either the product of the author's imagination or used fictitiously. Any resemblance to actual persons, living or dead, events, or locales is purely coincidental.

First Edition 2025

Publisher: MK Storyworks
Cover and Interior Design: MK Storyworks
Author: Carys Llewelyn

ISBN: 978-1-80700-034-9

TABLE OF CONTENTS

DEDICATION

For the seekers of invisible connections, and the brave who follow them.

A NOTE FROM THE AUTHOR

We are all connected by threads we cannot see. A shared glance, a moment of understanding, a sudden feeling of belonging, these are the whispers of a deeper tapestry.

This story was born from a desire to make those whispers visible. To imagine a world where the magic isn't in wands or spells, but in the quiet, luminous bonds between hearts. It's a story for anyone who has ever felt a pull toward a place, or a person, they couldn't logically explain.

Thank you for stepping into Asterly. I hope you find a little of its light stays with you.

— *Carys Llewelyn*

CHAPTER ONE

London was a ghost behind a veil of relentless rain. From her penthouse perch, Penelope Lowell watched the city's sharp edges dissolve into a monochrome haze. On the street below, a river of black umbrellas flowed endlessly, each one a shield against the downpour, and against any genuine connection. She never joined that current; she only ever observed its course.

A sip of cold espresso grounded her. Illuminated on her tablet screen, a multi-million-pound merger agreement lay open, its labyrinthine clauses a sanctuary of pure reason. This was the realm she understood: a world governed by the unyielding architecture of law and the clean, predictable burn of ambition. Emotions were statistical noise. Love was a critical flaw in the system, an unquantifiable variable that compromised every equation.

The phone's vibration against the ebony desk was an intrusion. An unknown number, a dialling code for a place called Asterly. The voice that answered was parchment-thin and formal, a relic speaking from a quieter world. A solicitor, a Mr. Sterling, delivering the news with calibrated grace: her great-aunt, Eleanor Lowell, had passed.

The name summoned a wisp of memory, the faint scent of lavender, a smile etched with kindness, from a single, long-ago summer. A file she had long since archived.

"As the sole beneficiary," the solicitor continued, "the property known as 'Sunlit Grove,' and all its assets, now belong to you."

Property. The word conjured visions of a dilapidated manor, a sinkhole for time and capital. An inconvenient complication.

"My assistant will handle the listing," Penelope declared, her fingers already composing the email to make it so.

A deliberate silence traveled down the line. "Naturally, Ms. Lowell. However, the will contains a specific condition. You are required to take physical possession. It is a necessary formality. You must... lay eyes on it."

A pointless excursion. A sentimental demand from beyond the grave. But Penelope Lowell was a master of closure. She would dispatch this obligation with her trademark, surgical efficiency.

Two days later, the sleek silence of her town car felt obscene on the winding lane into Asterly. The storm had surrendered, leaving a tentative sun to paint the cobblestones in gold. When she opened the door, the air itself was a revelation, a lush symphony of damp earth, wild honeysuckle, and a purity that scraped London from her lungs.

The village unfolded like an illustration from a forgotten storybook. Stone cottages slumped under the weight of floral explosions, a ancient bridge curved over a babbling stream, and a painted sign for The Weeping Willow groaned a weary welcome. It was meticulously charming, and to Penelope, utterly contrived.

Her navigation pointed beyond the square, but the key, the solicitor had insisted, was held at a bookshop.

The Folio & Hearth. The name was carved into weathered wood above a narrow door squeezed between a bakery and a post office. The window displayed a curated chaos: precarious stacks of leather-bound volumes, a brass globe tarnished with age, and a single, flawless orchid.

A delicate bell announced her entrance. The atmosphere within was a tangible thing, a hallowed blend of decaying paper, polished leather, and beeswax. It was the scent of silence itself. For one fleeting, profound moment, the frantic static in Penelope's mind hushed.

Then, a voice, rugged as river stone, shattered the peace.

"We're closed."

A man emerged from a canyon of shelves devoted to regional histories. He moved with the unstudied ease of physical labor, tall and solidly built. His hair was a thick, unruly wave of dark chestnut, and his eyes, the shade of a storm-laden sky, assessed her with bare annoyance. His flannel shirt, worn soft and rolled to the elbows, revealed forearms etched with the faint silver lines of old scars.

"It's half-past two," she stated, her voice a cool, polished instrument.

"And I'm closing at half-past two," he countered, not budging. His gaze traveled over her, a slow, deliberate audit of her designer heels, her severe coat, the impeccable knot of her hair. It was not a look of curiosity, but of judgment. "Can I help you, or are you just here to evaluate the clutter?"

She drew herself up to her full height, a posture reserved for intimidating rivals. "I'm here for the key to Sunlit Grove. I was directed to a Mr. Penrose."

His already guarded expression turned to flint. A deep furrow carved itself between his brows. He crossed his arms, the gesture a silent, impenetrable wall.

"The niece," he said. The words were an accusation, not a welcome.

"Penelope Lowell." She kept her hands at her sides.

He allowed the silence to swell, dense and charged with unspoken history. "Rhys Penrose. It's in the back." He turned and was swallowed by the shop's deeper gloom.

Rooted in place, she felt the chill of his animosity. As her vision acclimated to the soft, dusty light, she saw it.

A glimmer at the edge of sight. A single, luminous strand of silver, hanging in the air between a high beam and the space he had just occupied. It shimmered with an otherworldly light. She blinked, and the vision dissolved.

Fatigue, her intellect insisted, a swift, logical correction. *A phantom cast by strained eyes.*

But when Rhys returned, pressing the heavy, cold iron key into her palm without a word, the echo of it remained. The thread had vanished, yet a new, resonant frequency hummed in the air around them. And its source seemed to be the infuriating, brooding man who now held the door open, his silence a more potent dismissal than any shout.

CHAPTER TWO

The iron key was a cold, dead weight in Penelope's palm, its teeth biting into her skin. She stood on the gravel drive outside Sunlit Grove, staring up at the house that was now, inexplicably, hers.

It was not the crumbling ruin she had anticipated.

It was a poem written in stone and ivy. A two-story Georgian manor, its symmetry softened by a cascade of dark green vines that climbed the honey-colored stone. Mullioned windows winked in the afternoon light, and a sage-green door, painted the color of the surrounding woods, seemed to invite her in with quiet dignity. It was not derelict; it was dormant. Waiting.

Her logical mind scrambled for purchase. Well-maintained asset. Excellent condition. Higher property value than anticipated. But the thoughts rang hollow, feeble echoes in the profound quiet that surrounded this place. The air here was different from the village, thicker, sweeter, humming with a vibration she could feel in her teeth, in her bones.

Two hours. That's how long it had been since Rhys Penrose's cold dismissal in the bookshop, his grey eyes assessing her like she was a threat to something precious. The drive from the village square had taken less than ten minutes, but the landscape had shifted dramatically, from quaint cobblestones to this isolated grove, the woods pressing close on three sides, the house a elegant sentinel in the center.

Penelope took a breath and approached the sage-green door. The key turned in the lock with a solid, satisfying clunk. The interior greeted her with a sigh of dust and dried lavender. A wide hallway stretched before her, floorboards of dark oak gleaming where shafts of sunlight cut through the tall windows. A grandfather clock stood silent in the corner, its brass pendulum motionless, frozen at twenty past three. To the left, through an arched doorway, a parlor; to the right, a dining room; straight ahead, the promise of more rooms, more secrets.

It was the silence that unnerved her most. Not an empty silence, but a watchful one. Expectant. As if the house itself was holding its breath.

Driven by a composure she didn't quite feel, Penelope began a methodical inspection. The parlor held Victorian furniture draped in dust covers, a velvet settee, wing-backed chairs, side tables that would fetch excellent prices at auction. The dining room's mahogany table could seat twelve. The kitchen was a museum piece: porcelain sink, cast-iron stove, copper pots hanging from ceiling hooks, everything spotlessly clean despite obvious age.

But there were no photographs. No personal trinkets. No signs of the woman who had lived here for what must have been decades. Eleanor Lowell had left behind beautiful objects but no footprints, no evidence of a life lived. Only perfection, carefully preserved.

A small study branched off the kitchen, its walls lined with books. Penelope ran her fingers along the spines: local histories, botanical guides, volumes on folklore and mythology. A single, well-worn leather armchair sat by the window, positioned to overlook the back garden. This, she thought, was where Eleanor spent her time. Reading. Watching.

Through the window, the wild garden unfurled in glorious abandon. Roses had escaped their beds and tangled with lavender. Stone paths disappeared beneath drifts of forget-me-nots. Beyond the garden, woods so dense they seemed to swallow the daylight whole.

And at the tree line, a figure.

Rhys Penrose.

He stood motionless, hands in his pockets, his posture rigid. He wasn't looking at the house; he was staring into the woods, as if standing guard. Or keeping vigil.

Before Penelope could process this, something else seized her attention.

Movement in the garden, small, ordinary movements. Two sparrows chasing each other through the rose bushes. A bee burrowing into lavender. A blackbird perched on the garden wall.

And connecting them all: threads of light.

They bloomed into visibility as she watched, as if her focus had turned on some inner switch. A brilliant amethyst cord connected the two sparrows. A soft, buttery gold strand linked the bee to the lavender. Silver threads wove through the garden like a spider's web, connecting flowers to earth, branches to trunk, stone to moss. They were everywhere, a breathtaking tapestry of connection woven through the very fabric of the grove, invisible until this moment, now devastatingly, impossibly visible.

It was not a trick of the light. It was not stress or fatigue or grief manifesting as hallucination.

It was real.

Penelope stumbled backward from the window, her breath coming short. This was impossible. Threads of light didn't exist. Magic didn't exist. She was a lawyer. She dealt in evidence, in documentation, in facts that could be proven in court.

And yet.

Her hand found the window frame, steadying herself. When she looked again, the threads remained. If anything, they were brighter now, more defined. She could see the subtle differences in color, gold for some connections, silver for others, violet for others still. Each thread pulsing gently, like a heartbeat. Like they were alive.

A movement pulled her focus back to Rhys. He had turned from the woods and was now looking directly at her window. He couldn't possibly see her clearly through the sun-glazed glass, but she felt the weight of his gaze nonetheless. And from this distance, in the full light of the sun-dappled grove, she saw it clearly:

A single, gossamer-thin filament of light, the color of a newborn dawn, stretching from the center of his chest, across the wild garden, through the air, directly toward...

Toward her.

The key fell from her trembling hand, clattering loudly on the oak floor, the sound unnaturally loud in the watchful silence. She stood frozen, staring at that dawn-colored thread, her heart hammering. It was real. Undeniable. A connection between her and the hostile bookseller she'd met three hours ago, visible as anything she'd ever seen in her life.

A sharp knock at the front door made her jump.

Penelope retrieved the fallen key with shaking hands, forced herself to breathe, to think. Another hallucination? No, the threads were still visible when she glanced back at the garden. She was either genuinely seeing something impossible, or she was having a complete psychological breakdown.

The knock came again.

She walked to the front door, grateful for something concrete to focus on. Through the frosted glass, she could make out a feminine silhouette.

She opened the door to find a woman in her fifties, flour dusting her cardigan, her round face creased with genuine warmth.

"Oh, you must be Miss Lowell! I'm Maeve Brennan, from the bakery in the village." The woman's accent was local, her smile automatic. "I wanted to welcome you properly. Your aunt was such a dear friend." She thrust forward a cloth-covered basket. "Scones. Still warm."

"That's very kind," Penelope heard herself say, accepting the basket. The scent of butter and berries was intoxicating, grounding. Real.

"I won't keep you, I'm sure you're exhausted from the journey." Maeve's eyes were assessing but not unkind, taking in Penelope's tailored coat, her severe posture, the obvious tension in her shoulders. "But if you need anything, truly anything, the entire village is at your service. Eleanor was... well, she was the heart of this place."

"I appreciate that," Penelope replied, the words feeling inadequate.

Maeve lingered on the doorstep, her fingers worrying the edge of her cardigan. "I know Rhys can seem a bit... prickly. But he loved your aunt dearly. We all did. This has been hard on him especially." She paused, choosing her words carefully. "Give him time. He'll come around. Eleanor would have wanted you two to work together."

Work together? On what?

But Maeve was already departing with a final, encouraging nod, leaving Penelope alone with a basket of scones and more questions than answers.

She returned to the kitchen and set the basket on the scarred oak table. The scones were perfect, golden, studded with berries, still radiating warmth. She broke one open, watched the steam rise, and froze.

A thread. Pale gold, delicate as spider silk, extending from the scone in her hand through the kitchen wall, across the distance, all the way back to the village square. To the bakery.

To Maeve.

It wasn't just the garden. It wasn't just Rhys. Everything was connected. The food to its maker. The land to its inhabitants. And she, standing in the center of this impossible web, could suddenly perceive every luminous strand.

Penelope set the scone down with trembling hands. The lawyer in her demanded evidence, required proof that this wasn't madness. But the evidence was all around her, glowing in the late afternoon sun filtering through the kitchen window.

She thought of the silver thread she'd glimpsed in the bookshop, hanging in the air where Rhys had stood. She thought of the threads connecting him to the woods. And she remembered, with a chill that had nothing to do with temperature, that dawn-colored thread stretching between them like a bridge.

Whatever this was, whatever she was seeing, Rhys Penrose knew about it. He'd looked at her not with contempt, but with something else. Recognition, perhaps. Or fear. Fear of what she might be. Fear of what she might do.

The solicitor's words echoed in her memory: You are required to take physical possession. You must lay eyes on it.

Not on the house.

On this. On the light.

Penelope walked back to the entrance hall, to the door she'd noticed earlier, tucked under the staircase, almost invisible, made of the same dark wood as the paneling. She'd tried the key earlier; it hadn't worked. Now she placed her palm flat against the wood and felt it: warmth, pulse, a heartbeat in the bones of the house.

"What are you?" she whispered.

The wood beneath her hand thrummed once, subtle but unmistakable.

Outside, in the wild garden, Rhys Penrose turned from his vigil and looked directly at the kitchen window where she'd stood minutes before. The dawn-pink thread between them brightened, visible even in the daylight, and for one crystalline moment, Penelope understood.

She wasn't just the inheritor of a property.

She was the inheritor of a gift, or perhaps a burden.

And the brooding guardian at the tree line wasn't her enemy.

He was the only one who could teach her how to survive it.

Penelope walked to the front door and opened it. The compulsion was undeniable, she needed answers, and the man standing in her garden was the only one who had them.

Rhys was already approaching the house, his footsteps crunching on the gravel path. He stopped at the bottom of the front steps, maintaining a respectful distance.

"You saw them," he said. Not a question.

"I saw... something. Threads. Light." Her voice was steadier than she felt. "And you know what they are."

He nodded slowly. "I do. But this isn't a conversation for exhaustion and shock. You've had enough for one day." He glanced at the sky, where the afternoon was fading into evening. "I'll come back tomorrow morning. Eight AM. We'll talk then. I'll bring coffee."

"How do you..."

"Everyone needs coffee the morning after they first See." A ghost of a smile. "Especially lawyers."

Before she could respond, he turned and walked back toward the tree line, leaving her with a thousand questions and the certainty that tomorrow, at least some of them would be answered.

Penelope stood on the threshold of Sunlit Grove as the sun sank low, painting the wild garden in shades of amber and rose. The threads were still visible, pulsing gently in the fading light.

Tomorrow she would get answers.

Tonight, she would simply try to survive the impossibility of what she'd seen.

She closed the door and leaned against it, the iron key still clutched in her hand.

The house hummed around her, welcoming.

And in the oak grove beyond the garden, something ancient and powerful pulsed once in recognition.

Its new Seer had arrived.

CHAPTER THREE

The knock came at eight the next morning.

Penelope had not slept. She'd spent the night in Eleanor's study, wrapped in a throw blanket she'd found in a linen closet, staring out at the garden. Watching the threads pulse and shift in the moonlight. Trying to convince herself she was hallucinating. Failing.

When dawn finally broke, painting the wild garden in shades of rose and gold, she'd made coffee in Eleanor's ancient percolator and sat at the kitchen table with her phone, staring at the seven missed calls from her office. The Morrison merger didn't matter. Nothing in London mattered. Not anymore.

Because she could see threads of light connecting everything and everyone, and she had absolutely no idea what that meant.

The knock, when it came, was firm but not aggressive. She knew who it would be before she opened the door.

Rhys Penrose stood on the step, dressed in the same worn flannel and jeans as yesterday, carrying two takeaway cups of coffee and looking like he'd slept about as well as she had.

"May I come in?" he asked, his voice rough. Not hostile this time. Resigned.

She stepped aside.

He entered Sunlit Grove and stopped in the entrance hall, his gaze sweeping the space with obvious familiarity. "You saw them, didn't you? The threads."

"I don't know what I saw."

"Yes, you do." He handed her one of the coffee cups, black, no sugar, how did he know?, and moved toward the kitchen without waiting for permission. "Your aunt made the best coffee. This is from the village café. Not quite as good, but it'll do."

Penelope followed him, irritation warring with desperate curiosity. "You were watching the house last night. I saw you in the woods."

"I was keeping vigil." Rhys set his cup on the kitchen table, the same table where Eleanor had no doubt sat thousands of times. "Making sure you were all right. The first night in this house can be... overwhelming. Especially for someone with the Sight."

"The Sight."

"The ability to see the threads. The connections." He pulled out a chair, sat, gestured for her to do the same. "It runs in certain bloodlines. Your great-aunt Eleanor had it. My grandfather had it. And apparently, you have it too."

Penelope remained standing, her mind already cataloging arguments, rational explanations. "This is insane. Threads of light don't exist. Magic doesn't..."

"Magic is just a word for phenomena we don't fully understand," Rhys interrupted. "Call it magic, call it quantum entanglement made visible, call it whatever makes you comfortable. The point is: you can see it. Which means you're a Seer."

"No." Penelope stood abruptly. "This is insane. I need to call my doctor. This could be stress-induced psychosis, a tumor, temporal lobe epilepsy..."

"You're not hallucinating."

"You don't know that. I've been under enormous pressure. The inheritance, this house..." She pulled out her phone. "I'm scheduling an MRI."

"Penelope. Look at your hand."

She looked. The dawn-colored thread was still there, pulsing between them. She closed her eyes. It didn't disappear.

"This isn't real," she whispered.

"It is. And you know it." Rhys's voice was steady. "You saw the threads multiple times yesterday. In my shop. In the garden. Consistent phenomena under varying conditions. Apply your legal mind. What's the simplest explanation?"

"That I'm having a psychotic break."

"Or that you're seeing something real that most people can't see. Something your aunt saw her entire life." He gestured to the window. "Test it. Look at the village. Tell me what you see."

Against her better judgment, Penelope moved to the window. Opened herself to the sight. The threads blazed into view. Golden connections between houses. Silver bonds linking the church. Bronze strands between the pub and bakery.

"The threads are denser in the village center," she heard herself say. "Thinner at the edges. They follow social bonds. That house has almost no threads. Someone isolated."

"Mrs. Patterson. Widow. Moved here six months ago."

"And that one is brilliant with connections."

"The Morrison family. Four generations."

Penelope's breath caught. If this was hallucination, it wouldn't predict social structures she knew nothing about. If this was delusion, it wouldn't correlate with reality.

"I'm seeing something real," she whispered.

"Yes."

"A Seer."

"Someone who can perceive the Tethering Light. The web of connections that binds people, places, things. Most people go their whole lives never knowing it exists. They feel it, they say 'we have chemistry' or 'this place feels like home' or 'I'm drawn to this person', but they can't see the actual threads. You can."

Penelope finally sat, more because her legs were shaking than because she wanted to. "And you? Can you see them?"

"No. Not the way you do." Rhys's expression was difficult to read. "I can sense them. Feel them when they're strong. My grandfather called me a potential Guardian, someone who can work with a Seer, anchor them, protect them from getting lost in the network. But I don't have the Sight itself."

"This is..." Penelope struggled for words. "This is absolutely insane."

"And yet you know it's true." His grey eyes were steady, certain. "Because you saw them. Multiple times yesterday. The threads in my shop. The threads in the garden. And you saw the one connecting you to me. Dawn-colored gold. That's a Guardian bond. When a Seer and a Guardian are compatible, when they could potentially work together, the thread appears. Eleanor and my grandfather had one. It was how they protected this place for forty years."

"Protected it from what?"

Rhys was quiet for a moment, choosing his words. "The threads are weakening. Everywhere. For decades, centuries maybe, the world has been moving toward disconnection. People leave communities for cities. Families fracture. Old bonds break and new ones don't form to replace them. Each severed connection weakens the network. And when the network weakens..." He gestured at the house, the grove beyond. "Places like this suffer."

"Places like this."

"Asterly has a Heartstone. The heart of the thread network for this region. It's in the oak grove beyond the garden; you probably felt its pull yesterday. It's what makes this village what it is. What maintains the connections between people, between the land and its inhabitants. Your great-aunt was its guardian. She kept it safe, maintained the threads, mended breaks when they occurred. For forty-three years, she was the reason this place stayed connected, stayed whole."

Penelope absorbed this, her lawyer's mind already poking holes. "If she was so powerful, why did she need a Guardian?"

"Because using the Sight alone, without an anchor, burns you out. Drains you." Rhys's voice roughened. "My grandfather died when Eleanor was fifty-eight. She spent the next ten years trying to protect the Heartstone alone. It aged her rapidly. Wore her down. By the end, she looked ancient, though she was only sixty-eight when she died."

"And she left this to me. This... burden." Penelope heard the bitterness in her own voice. "Why? I met her once when I was seven. She didn't know me."

"The Sight runs in bloodlines. You were the only family she had left. And the Heartstone chose you, it reacted when you arrived in the village. That's not something that happens randomly." Rhys leaned forward, his expression intent. "Whether you want this or not, Penelope, you've inherited it. The question is: will you accept it? Will you learn to use the Sight properly, to protect what Eleanor spent her life maintaining? Or will you walk away and let it all unravel?"

The weight of his words settled over her like snow. This was impossible. Insane. Everything she'd built her life to avoid, vague responsibilities, unquantifiable commitments, faith in things that couldn't be proven.

And yet.

"That thread," she heard herself say. "The dawn-colored one. Between us. You said it means we could work together."

"Could. Not must. The thread shows compatibility, potential. What we do with it, whether we develop that partnership or ignore it, that's up to us."

"And if I refuse? If I sell this house and go back to London?"

Rhys's jaw tightened. "Then the Heartstone weakens. The threads in Asterly begin to fray. Within a generation, maybe two, this place becomes just another village that young people leave and old people die in. The connections that make it special, the bonds between families, the relationship between land and community, all of it dissolves. It becomes forgettable. Generic. Dead."

"That's not fair. You can't put that responsibility on me..."

"I'm not putting it on you. Eleanor did. The Heartstone did. I'm just explaining what you've inherited." He stood, picking up his coffee cup. "I'll give you time to think. But think quickly. Because there are people, companies, organizations, who would very much like to acquire this property. And they don't want to preserve the Heartstone. They want to destroy it."

"Why would anyone want to destroy it?"

"Because connection is unpredictable. Messy. It makes people loyal to each other instead of to profit. It makes them value communities over careers, relationships over transactions." His expression darkened. "There are forces in this world that profit from disconnection. From severing bonds. From turning everything into a commodity. And they've been very successful at it."

He moved toward the door, then stopped. "For what it's worth, Eleanor believed you could do this. She left everything, her research, her journals, her entire life's work, for you. She thought you were strong enough to carry it. Whether you believe that is up to you."

"Wait." Penelope stood, her coffee forgotten. "If I... if I decide to try this. To learn. Would you help me?"

Rhys turned back, and for the first time since she'd met him, she saw something other than hostility or resignation in his eyes. Hope, perhaps. Or relief.

"Yes," he said simply. "That's what the Guardian bond means. If you'll accept it."

"I don't accept anything," Penelope said, her voice sharper than she intended. "Not yet. But I'm willing to learn. To understand what this is before I make any decisions."

"That's enough." A slight smile tugged at his mouth. "We'll continue tomorrow. Same time. I'll bring breakfast. And Penelope..." He paused at the door. "Don't use the Sight extensively until I'm here to guide you. It's easy to get lost, especially at first. Promise me."

"I don't make promises to people I barely know."

"Then make it to yourself. Because if you get lost in the thread network, I might not be able to pull you back. Not until the Guardian bond is stronger."

He left before she could respond, the door closing with a soft click behind him.

Penelope stood in Eleanor's entrance hall, a cold cup of coffee in her hand, staring at the space where Rhys had been. Where that dawn-colored thread still hung in the air, invisible to him but blazing bright to her.

She had two choices: run back to London and pretend this had never happened, or stay and learn to navigate a world that operated according to rules she'd never imagined existed.

Her phone buzzed. Another call from her office. The Morrison merger. Her real life, her real career, everything she'd worked a decade to build.

She let it go to voicemail.

And began to climb the stairs toward Eleanor's attic, where, if Rhys was right, she would find the research, the journals, the answers to questions she hadn't known to ask.

The house thrummed around her, approving.

Outside, in the oak grove beyond the wild garden, the Heartstone pulsed once.

Waiting.

CHAPTER FOUR

The attic stairs were narrow and steep, made for servants in another century. Penelope climbed them in the late afternoon light, her heart still hammering from Rhys's revelations and the impossible things she'd seen.

A Seer. The Sight. Guardian bonds and Heartstones and a network of connections that held communities together. It sounded like fantasy, like the kind of nonsense she'd spent her entire adult life dismissing.

Except she could see it. The threads. Even now, even trying not to look, she could sense them at the edges of her vision, connections between the house and the land, between rooms and memories, between her and this place she'd never meant to claim.

The attic door was hidden behind a false wall on the second floor landing, the kind of clever Victorian construction meant to create secret spaces. She'd found it by accident, her hand brushing the wallpaper and feeling it give slightly. Now it swung open to reveal a finished attic space that Eleanor had clearly used as her study.

Books lined every available surface. But these weren't the local histories and botanical guides from downstairs. These were grimoires, bestiaries, illuminated manuscripts that belonged in museum collections. Astrological charts covered one wall. Another held what looked like a genealogical tree, but instead of names, there were symbols she didn't recognize: spirals, stars, interlocking circles.

And in the center of the room, on a pedestal made of three stacked stones, sat a small Heartstone.

Penelope stopped in the doorway, transfixed.

It was smaller than she'd expected, no larger than her fist, but it pulsed with the same pearl-like luminescence she'd seen in the garden threads. Golden threads radiated from it like spokes on a wheel, stretching out through the walls, through the floor, disappearing into distances she couldn't fathom.

This, she understood with sudden clarity, was the heart of it all. The source. What Eleanor had protected for forty-three years. What Rhys was asking her to protect now.

She forced herself to step closer.

A desk sat beneath one of the dormer windows, its surface covered with papers, journals, astronomical equipment. One journal lay open, Eleanor's elegant handwriting covering the page:

June 14th, 1998

Thomas died today. The bond between us severed cleanly, like a cut thread. I felt it the moment his heart stopped. And now I am alone with the Heartstone, with no Guardian to anchor me, and I don't know how long I can maintain this without him.

I have perhaps ten years. Maybe fifteen if I'm careful. After that, the Sight will consume me, or age will. Either way, I must find a successor before then. Someone with the bloodline. Someone strong enough to carry this burden.

Penelope turned the page.

June 20th, 1998

I've been thinking about my great-niece. Penelope. I met her only once, when she was seven. Sharp as a blade even then, asking questions no child should know to ask. She has the eyes. That particular grey-green that runs in our family, the color of storm clouds before rain. The Sight is in her. Dormant, perhaps. But there.

If I can hold on long enough, if I can survive until she's ready, I will leave her everything. The Grove, the Heartstone, my journals, my research. And I will pray that she's strong enough to do what I could not: find her Guardian and protect this place properly. Together.

The entry ended there.

Penelope stood in Eleanor's attic, holding the journal, her vision blurring with tears she couldn't explain. Eleanor had known. Had planned this. Had spent the last ten years of her life keeping the Heartstone alive long enough to pass it to someone who might succeed where she'd failed.

The weight of that sacrifice, that hope, settled over Penelope's shoulders like a mantle.

She pulled out the desk chair and sat, wiping her eyes angrily. She didn't cry. Hadn't cried since she was a teenager. Certainly didn't cry over a relative she'd barely known and a magical responsibility she'd never asked for.

But the tears kept coming anyway.

Outside, in the wild garden, the late afternoon sun began its slow descent. And in the oak grove beyond, the larger Heartstone pulsed in rhythm with its smaller twin, waiting for its new guardian to accept her inheritance.

Penelope lost track of time in Eleanor's attic. She read journal after journal, each entry revealing more about the Tethering Light, about the network of connections, about the loneliness of maintaining it alone. Eleanor had been methodical, documenting everything: which families had the strongest bonds, which places in the village were nexus points for threads, how the Heartstone's pulse changed with the seasons.

By the time footsteps sounded on the attic stairs, twilight had painted the sky in shades of violet and rose.

"Penelope?" Rhys's voice, cautious.

She looked up, startled. "How did you get in?"

"You left the front door unlocked." He stood at the top of the stairs, taking in the attic, the journals spread across the desk, her tear-stained face. "I was worried when you didn't answer your phone."

She glanced at her mobile, forgotten on the desk. Seven missed calls. "I was reading."

"I can see that." He moved closer, his gaze sweeping over Eleanor's collection. "This was her sanctuary. I used to bring her tea up here when she was working. She'd get so absorbed she'd forget to eat."

"She was alone for ten years. After your grandfather died."

"Yes." His voice was soft. "And it destroyed her, slowly. That's why I need you to understand what you're taking on. This work, it can't be done alone. Not for long."

Penelope stood, her legs stiff from sitting. "You said tomorrow morning. Training."

"I did. But that was before I realized you'd spend the entire afternoon up here." He studied her face. "You've decided to stay, haven't you?"

"I have to. Eleanor gave up everything for this. I can't just walk away." She gestured at the journals. "But I need to learn properly. I need you to teach me how to do this without burning out like she did."

"That's why the Guardian bond exists." The dawn-colored thread between them pulsed, visible in the dimming light. "But we need to start slowly. Build your control before we attempt anything difficult."

"How slowly?"

"A few days of basic training. Then, if you're ready, we'll try something real." He moved to the window, looking out at the darkening village. "There's a situation developing. Two men, business partners for twenty years. Their relationship is fracturing. The thread between them is turning from bronze to sickly yellow. If it breaks completely, it'll damage the network. Small damage, but damage nonetheless."

"And you want me to try to fix it."

"I want you to try to strengthen it. To remind them why they connected in the first place." He turned back to her. "But not yet. First, you learn control. Then, we practice on stable threads. Only after that do we attempt repairs."

Penelope nodded slowly. "When does their thread break?"

"Three days, maybe four. We have time."

"Then we start tomorrow morning. Eight o'clock?"

"Eight o'clock. I'll bring breakfast." His slight smile returned. "And you should sleep. Actual sleep, in an actual bed, not up here in a dusty attic."

She realized how exhausted she was. The emotional weight of the day, the hours of reading, the tears. "You're right."

They descended the narrow stairs together, the house settling into nighttime silence around them. At the front door, Rhys paused.

"Penelope. What you're doing, accepting this burden. Eleanor would be proud."

"I hope so." She met his eyes. "Because I'm terrified."

"Good. Fear means you understand what's at stake." He stepped out into the night. "See you tomorrow. Get some rest."

After he left, Penelope locked the door and climbed the main stairs to the bedroom she'd chosen. Eleanor's room, with its four-poster bed and windows overlooking the oak grove. She fell asleep within minutes, exhausted.

And dreamed of golden threads connecting everything.

The next three days passed in a blur of training.

Rhys arrived each morning at eight with coffee and pastries from Maeve's bakery. They worked in Eleanor's study, the one room that felt neither too formal nor too intimate. He taught her to narrow her focus, to look at single threads instead of being overwhelmed by the entire network.

It was harder than she'd anticipated. Every time she opened the Sight, hundreds of connections blazed into view, each one demanding attention. Learning to isolate one thread felt like trying to listen to a single violin in an orchestra.

But she improved. By the second day, she could hold focus on a single thread for five full minutes. By the third day, ten minutes without losing herself.

"You're ready," Rhys said on the afternoon of the third day.

"For what?"

"To try a real intervention. The situation I mentioned. It's come to a head. They're meeting in the village square in an hour. Liam Patel and Benjamin Harrison. Twenty-year business partnership, currently fracturing over something stupid."

Penelope's stomach dropped. "An hour? That's not much warning."

"Welcome to being a Seer. Threads don't break on convenient schedules." He stood, offering his hand. "But you can do this. I'll be right there, anchoring you. And if it goes wrong, we pull back and try a different approach."

She took his hand, feeling the dawn-colored thread between them pulse with warmth and certainty. "What if I make it worse?"

"You won't. Trust yourself. And trust the bond."

They walked to the village square as the afternoon sun slanted long and golden across the cobblestones. A small crowd had gathered outside Mrs. Bramble's tea shop, watching two men argue in increasingly heated tones.

Liam Patel was stocky and red-faced, gesturing wildly. Benjamin Harrison stood rigid, his jaw clenched, fists at his sides. The anger between them was palpable even without the Sight.

"What are they arguing about?" Penelope whispered.

"A contract dispute. Liam bid on a project without consulting Ben. Ben found out and accused him of going behind his back. It's escalated from there." Rhys positioned them at the edge of the crowd. "Open the Sight. Look at their thread."

Penelope took a breath and focused. The world burst into threads of light. She narrowed her vision, searching for the connection between the two men.

There. A thread that should have been bronze with partnership and trust, now a sickly yellow-green. Fraying. With each angry word, tiny filaments snapped away, weakening the bond.

"I see it," she murmured.

"Good. Now look deeper. Past the damage. There's always a core strand. The original reason they connected. Find that."

She focused harder, pushing past the frayed yellow outer layers. And there, buried beneath years of accumulated stress and resentment, a thin copper strand. Bright and clean. The original friendship. The trust that had made them partners in the first place.

"I found it."

"Can you strengthen it?"

"I don't know how."

"You do. You just don't know you know." Rhys's voice was steady, grounding. "Remember what I taught you. Intent matters. Will matters. You don't manipulate the thread directly. You remind it what it was. What it should be."

Penelope reached out, not with her hands but with her will, her intention. She touched the thin copper strand with her consciousness.

Remember, she thought. *Remember why you were friends. Remember twenty years of success. Remember trust.*

The copper strand pulsed.

Once.

Twice.

Then it began to grow. To thicken. Drawing the frayed yellow filaments back toward its core, weaving them into something stronger. The sickly color shifted toward bronze, warming, glowing.

In the square, Liam's voice faltered. "I... Look, Ben, I'm sorry. I should have called you before submitting that bid. You're right. It was wrong."

Ben's rigid posture softened. "And I shouldn't have accused you of cheating. I know you wouldn't. Twenty years, mate. We don't throw that away over one mistake."

The crowd began to disperse as the two men shook hands, then pulled each other into a brief, awkward hug.

Penelope released the thread and stumbled. Rhys caught her elbow, steadying her.

"Easy. First real mending always hits hard."

"Did I do that?" Her voice sounded distant to her own ears.

"You did. You mended a twenty-year partnership in about ninety seconds." He guided her to a bench. "Sit. Catch your breath."

Mrs. Bramble appeared with a glass of water. Maeve brought a scone. The villagers who'd witnessed the argument nodded their thanks as they passed.

They knew. They understood what she'd done, even if they couldn't see the threads themselves.

"How do you feel?" Rhys asked.

"Dizzy. Exhausted. But..." She looked at her hands, still trembling. "I did it. I actually did it."

"You did. And Liam and Ben's friendship is stronger for it." He sat beside her. "This is what Seers do, Penelope. We don't just see the connections. We protect them. Maintain them. Fight for them when they're threatened."

She watched the two men walk away together, already talking about their next project, the argument forgotten. The bronze thread between them glowed steady and strong.

"The training begins," she said quietly.

"The training began three days ago." Rhys smiled. "This was your first field test. And you passed."

Penelope drank the water, ate the scone, and felt the exhaustion begin to ebb. Her first real intervention. Her first mended thread.

The first of many.

CHAPTER FIVE

Three days of training, and Penelope's world had been turned inside out.

Three days of sitting in Eleanor's study with Rhys, learning to focus the Sight on single threads instead of being overwhelmed by the entire network. Three days of headaches that left her dizzy and nauseous. Three days of Rhys's steady voice talking her back from the edge when the threads threatened to consume her entirely.

But they were making progress.

On the third morning, Penelope managed to hold focus on a single thread for ten full minutes. A silver connection between Mrs. Bramble and her tea shop, glowing steady and strong. She could see the decades of care woven into it, the thousands of customers served, the community meetings hosted, the quiet acts of kindness that had built the bond between woman and place.

When she released it, she wasn't dizzy. Wasn't lost. Just

tired.

"You're getting better," Rhys said, watching her from Eleanor's leather armchair. "Eleanor took two weeks to manage this level of control."

"Eleanor didn't spend ten years training herself to see only facts and evidence," Penelope muttered, rubbing her temples. "I'm having to unlearn a decade of thinking before I can learn this."

"That's actually an advantage. Your analytical mind helps you categorize what you're seeing. Most Seers just get lost in the emotional overwhelm."

She looked at him, sitting there with afternoon light gilding his dark hair, and felt the now familiar tug of the dawn gold thread between them. It was stronger every day they worked together. Brighter. More defined.

After he'd explained everything about the Tethering Light, after she'd spent days in Eleanor's attic reading journals and weeping over her great aunt's sacrifice, she'd made a decision.

Not just to learn the Sight. Not just to protect the Heartstone. But to commit fully to this life.

Which meant closing her old one.

"I need to go to London," she said abruptly.

Rhys looked up from the book he'd been reading. "What?"

"I need to resign properly. Handle my cases. Close my

apartment. I can't keep straddling two worlds. If I'm going to be a Seer, if I'm going to protect Asterly, I need to do it completely. No safety net. No fallback plan."

"Are you sure? Penelope, you've only been here a week. That's not much time to make such a permanent choice."

"I know. But I also know that if I don't do this now, if I leave any door open to my old life, I'll convince myself this was temporary madness. I'll go back to London and pretend the threads don't exist. Pretend I never saw the Heartstone." She stood, pacing. "I need to burn the bridges. Make this choice irreversible."

Through the dawn gold thread, she felt his conflict. His fear that she'd regret this. His hope that she wouldn't. His deep, bone certain relief that she was choosing to stay.

"How long will you need?" he asked quietly.

"A week. Maybe less. Just long enough to resign, pack up the apartment, transfer my cases." She paused. "Will you be all right here? Watching the Heartstone alone?"

"I'm not a Seer, but I can monitor the basics. If anything, major happens, I'll call you immediately."

"And if something threatens the village while I'm gone? If developers come? If someone tries to pressure people to sell?"

"Then the village will deal with it. Penelope, we managed before you arrived. We'll manage for a week while you're gone."

She knew he was right. But the thought of leaving Asterly,

even briefly, felt wrong. As if the threads connecting her to this place were already so strong that distance would cause physical pain.

"I'll leave tomorrow morning," she decided. "That gives me today to show you how to monitor the Heartstone's basic rhythms. Make sure you can sense if threads start breaking."

They spent the afternoon in the oak grove. Rhys couldn't See the threads the way Penelope could, but he had sensitivity. Could feel when connections were healthy or strained. She taught him to place his hand on the Heartstone and sense the pulse of the network, the way a doctor might feel a patient's heartbeat.

"It's like... warmth," he said, his palm flat against the glowing stone. "When the threads are healthy, there's warmth. When they're damaged, it feels cold. Absent."

"Exactly. You won't be able to mend breaks, but you'll know when something needs attention. You can contact me, and I'll talk you through stabilizing it until I get back."

"Or I'll just tell the village to stop being idiots and repair their own relationships," Rhys said dryly. "Most thread damage comes from people being stubborn. Refusing to apologize. Letting small disagreements become major rifts."

"You can't just tell people to fix their relationships."

"Watch me."

Penelope laughed despite herself. The tension of the decision easing slightly. This was good. This was right. London for a week to close that chapter of her life, then back here. To Asterly. To Rhys. To work that mattered.

That evening, she called her senior partner.

Robert answered on the third ring. "Penelope. Finally. We need to talk about the Morrison merger. Jennifer's doing her best, but she doesn't have your background on the..."

"Robert, I'm resigning."

Silence.

Then, "I'm sorry, what?"

"My partnership. I'm resigning it. Effective immediately." She kept her voice steady, professional. "I'll be in London next week to handle the transition. I'll recommend Jennifer to take over all my active cases. She's more than capable."

"Penelope, this is insane. You can't just resign a partnership. There are contracts, obligations, clients who specifically requested you..."

"The partnership agreement allows resignation with two weeks notice. I'm giving you a week in person to transition, plus I'm willing to consult remotely on critical cases for the next month. After that, I'm done."

"Is this about your aunt's death? Because grief can cloud judgment, and if you need time off, we can arrange..."

"It's not grief, Robert. It's clarity. I've spent ten years building a career I thought I wanted. And I was wrong. I want something else now."

"What could possibly be better than a partnership at one of London's top firms?"

"A manor house in the Cotswolds. A village that actually needs me. Work that matters beyond billable hours and profit margins."

Another long silence. Then Robert sighed. "You know, I always thought you'd burn out eventually. Too driven, too perfect, too unwilling to show weakness. But I never imagined you'd chuck it all for village life."

"Neither did I."

"Will you at least stay on retainer? Handle the occasional case remotely? Penelope, you're too good at this to walk away completely."

She considered. The money would be useful. Manor upkeep wasn't cheap. And maintaining some connection to the legal world might prove valuable, especially if she needed to fight anyone threatening Asterly.

"Remote consultation only," she said finally. "No more than ten hours a week. And only cases that interest me. No more mergers and acquisitions unless there's a compelling reason."

"Done. I'll have the paperwork drawn up." He paused. "For what it's worth, I think you're making a mistake. But I also think you're probably happier than I've ever heard you. So maybe it's the right mistake."

After they hung up, Penelope sat in Eleanor's study, her

phone in her hand, and felt a weight lift. One bridge burned. The first of many.

The next morning, she packed a small bag and stood at Sunlit Grove's door, keys in hand. Rhys waited by his car to drive her to the train station.

"You'll come back," he said. It wasn't a question.

"I'll come back. I promise."

"Because if you don't, I'm coming to London to drag you back myself."

She laughed and kissed him. Quick and certain, the dawn gold thread blazing between them. "One week. Then I'm home."

Home. She'd said it without thinking, but it was true. Asterly was home now. London was just the place she needed to pack up and say goodbye to.

The train ride felt surreal. Watching the countryside give way to suburbs, then the grey sprawl of the city. Every mile taking her further from the threads she could see, the connections she understood. By the time she reached King's Cross, the visible network had faded entirely. London was too dense, too transient, too fractured for the Sight to penetrate clearly.

It was like going deaf.

Her apartment in Kensington felt like a museum when she unlocked the door. Everything exactly as she'd left it two weeks ago. White walls, minimal furniture, no photographs or personal touches. It could have belonged to anyone. A hotel room she'd been paying mortgage on for six years.

She spent the next three days dismantling her London life with surgical efficiency. Meeting with Robert to transition cases. Packing the few possessions she wanted to keep. Putting the apartment on the market. Notifying her gym, her dry cleaner, the handful of restaurants where she had standing reservations.

It was remarkable how little of it mattered.

On the fourth day, she met her mother for lunch.

Catherine Lowell arrived at the restaurant looking elegant and concerned. She embraced Penelope, then held her at arm's length, studying her face.

"You look different," she said.

"Different how?"

"Calmer. Happier. Less... brittle." Her mother smiled. "I like it. Whatever you're doing in that village, it agrees with you."

Over lunch, Penelope tried to explain. Not the magic, not the Sight, but the community. The sense of belonging. The work that felt meaningful.

"Your father thinks you've lost your mind," Catherine said, picking at her salad. "Throwing away a partnership for a village no one's heard of."

"And you?"

"I think you were never happy in London. You just didn't realize there were alternatives." Her mother reached across the table and squeezed her hand. "If this makes you happy, if you've found something worth protecting, then I'm proud of you."

Penelope felt her eyes sting with unexpected tears. "Thank you."

"Just promise me you'll visit occasionally. And call your mother more than once every three months."

"I promise."

On her last evening in London, Penelope stood at her apartment window looking out over the city. Millions of people, millions of connections, but none of them visible to her here. The network too damaged, too fragmented by isolation and transience.

Her phone buzzed. A text from Rhys: *How's London?*

She smiled and typed back: *Loud. Crowded. No threads visible at all. Missing the grove.*

His response came quickly: *The grove misses you too. Mrs. Bramble asked after you three times today. Maeve saved you scones.*

And you?

A longer pause. Then: *I miss you. Come home soon.*

The dawn gold thread between them pulsed, visible even here in thread-dead London. Brighter than it had been a week ago. Stronger. Distance hadn't weakened it. If anything, the separation had made her more aware of its importance.

Tomorrow, she typed. *I'm coming home tomorrow.*

She packed the last of her things that night. One suitcase of clothes. One box of books. Everything else either sold or donated. A decade of accumulation reduced to two pieces of luggage.

It felt like freedom.

The train ride back to the Cotswolds the next day felt like returning to the world after holding her breath underwater. The moment she crossed into Gloucestershire, the threads became visible again. Faint at first, then stronger as she approached Asterly.

By the time Rhys picked her up at the station, she could See the golden threads connecting the village to its land, its people to each other, everything woven together in beautiful complexity.

"Welcome home," Rhys said, and kissed her in the station car park with the late afternoon sun warming them both.

"It's good to be back."

As they drove through Asterly toward Sunlit Grove, Penelope noticed something different. New threads. Connections that hadn't existed a week ago. The Patels and the Harrisons, their friendship mended after she'd helped repair their heartline, now glowing bronze and strong. Mrs. Henderson and Maeve, a new silver thread forming from some shared project.

The village was maintaining itself. Growing stronger.

"What happened while I was gone?" she asked.

"People remembered what you showed them. About the threads, about connection mattering. They've been working on their relationships. Making amends. Building bridges." Rhys smiled. "You started something, Penelope. They're continuing it."

Back at Sunlit Grove, unpacking her meager possessions into Eleanor's house, Penelope understood something fundamental. She wasn't just protecting the Heartstone. She was teaching the village to protect itself. To value connection before it was threatened. To maintain the network through daily acts of kindness and reconciliation.

That was the real work of a Seer. Not dramatic interventions. Not heroic thread mending. But helping communities remember how to stay connected.

"Rhys," she said, finding him in the kitchen making tea. "We need to teach people. Not just in Asterly. Everywhere. How to value connection. How to maintain relationships. How to resist the isolation that makes them vulnerable."

"That's ambitious."

"So is protecting a global network of Heartstones. But someone has to do it."

He handed her a cup of tea and kissed her forehead. "Then let's get started."

That night, sitting in Eleanor's study with maps and notes spread across the desk, they began planning something larger than either had imagined. Not just protecting Asterly. Not just defending one village. But building a network that could teach communities everywhere to value connection. To resist severance.

It would take years. Maybe decades.

But Eleanor had protected one Heartstone for forty-three years. Surely they could manage protecting many.

Outside, in the oak grove, the Heartstone pulsed contentedly. Its Seer was home. Its threads were growing stronger. And something new was beginning.

CHAPTER SIX

A week after returning from London, Penelope woke to raised voices in the village square.

She dressed quickly and hurried down from Sunlit Grove. A crowd had gathered outside Mrs. Bramble's tea shop, their expressions worried. At the center stood a man Penelope had never seen before. Mid thirties, expensive suit, the kind of polished appearance that screamed corporate lawyer.

"Ms. Lowell." He extended his hand as she approached. "Marcus Thorne. I represent Omni Corporation. We've been very interested in this region."

Penelope didn't take his hand. "What do you want?"

"Direct. I like that." He pulled out a tablet, showed her photographs. Sunlit Grove. The oak grove. The village square. "Omni Corp specializes in heritage development. We transform historical villages into premium destinations. Tourism, luxury accommodation, artisan shopping. We believe Asterly has tremendous potential."

"Asterly isn't for sale."

"Everything's for sale at the right price, Ms. Lowell. We're prepared to make very generous offers to property owners. Life changing sums for most of these people." He gestured at the crowd. "Enough to retire comfortably. Move somewhere warmer. Finally take that dream vacation."

"You're not buying Sunlit Grove."

"I'm not here for Sunlit Grove. Not yet, anyway. We're starting with more... willing sellers. The Thomases, perhaps. I understand they have a grandson with expensive medical needs. Or the Hendersons. Retirement age, struggling with the costs of maintaining their post office. We can help these people, Ms. Lowell. Give them financial security."

"What you're offering isn't security. It's severance. You want to break apart this community, replace local businesses with corporate chains, turn Asterly into another generic tourist trap."

Thorne's smile didn't waver. "That's a very cynical view. We're offering economic development. Job creation. Infrastructure improvements. Most people see that as positive."

"Most people can't see what you're really destroying."

"And what's that?"

Penelope opened her Sight fully. The threads blazed visible around them. Hundreds of connections weaving through the village. Gold and silver and bronze and crimson. Generations of accumulated belonging.

She couldn't make Thorne see them. Didn't have that power yet. But she could see them herself, and it strengthened her resolve.

"You're destroying connection. Community. Everything that makes this place worth living in. And you know it. This isn't your first village. You've done this before."

Something flickered in Thorne's expression. Not guilt, but acknowledgment. "I'm a businessman, Ms. Lowell. Omni Corp pays me to acquire properties. What happens after acquisition isn't my concern. Now, I'll be speaking with individual property owners over the next few days. I suggest you don't interfere with legitimate business transactions."

He walked away, leaving behind a crowd of worried villagers.

Mrs. Bramble moved to stand beside Penelope. "Omni Corp. I've heard of them. They developed a village in Yorkshire two years ago. My cousin lived there. Said it changed completely. All the locals left. Now it's just holiday cottages and expensive tea shops for tourists."

"We need to organize," Penelope said. "Make sure everyone understands what they'd be giving up. Can you call a village meeting? Tonight?"

By evening, Sunlit Grove's dining room was packed. Thirty villagers crammed around Eleanor's long table and spilling into the hallway. Tom Thomas, the Patels, the Harrisons, Mrs. Henderson, Maeve. Everyone who'd been approached by Omni Corp, plus those who expected to be.

Penelope stood at the head of the table, Rhys beside her.

"Thank you for coming," she began. "I know Marcus Thorne has been making you offers. Large sums of money. Tempting sums. I'm not here to tell you not to sell. That's your choice. But I want to make sure you understand what you'd be selling."

She gestured to Rhys, who pulled up a laptop presentation. Images of other villages Omni Corp had developed. Before and after photographs showing charming local communities transformed into sterile developments.

"This is Woolton in Yorkshire," Rhys explained. "Before Omni Corp, it had a population of eight hundred. Strong local economy, families that had lived there for generations. After development, the population dropped to two hundred and fifty. Everyone else priced out or forced to relocate. Now it's mostly holiday lets and second homes."

"This is Millbrook in Cornwall," Penelope continued. "Three hundred year old fishing community. Omni Corp developed it into a luxury marina. The fishing families couldn't afford to stay. Now it's weekenders and retirees."

One after another, they showed examples. Villages gutted, communities fractured, local identity erased.

"Omni Corp calls it development," Penelope said. "But what they're really doing is severance. Cutting the connections that make these places communities instead of just collections of buildings."

Tom Thomas raised his hand. "I understand what you're saying. But Ms. Lowell, my grandson needs treatment that costs fifteen thousand pounds. The NHS will cover some, but not all. If Omni Corp offers me enough to pay for his care, how can I refuse? How can I choose the village over my family?"

The room went silent. Because he was right. Money

mattered. Medical care mattered. How could anyone argue against a grandfather trying to help his sick grandson?

Penelope felt her certainty waver. Then she opened the Sight and looked at Tom Thomas properly.

The threads connecting him to Asterly were intricate and deep. His family had lived here for six generations. Bronze threads to his workshop, where his grandfather and father had worked before him. Crimson threads to his children and grandchildren. Silver threads to dozens of neighbors, customers, friends. And beneath it all, a golden thread connecting him to the land itself, to centuries of accumulated belonging.

But there was another thread too. A new one, barely formed but growing. Connecting his grandson to the village. To Mrs. Bramble, who'd organized the medical fund. To Maeve, who brought meals every week. To the Patels, who'd given the family free groceries during the worst months. To dozens of people who'd contributed money, time, support.

"Tom," Penelope said gently. "How much has the village raised for your grandson's treatment?"

He looked surprised by the question. "Eleven thousand so far. People have been incredibly generous."

"And how much more do you need?"

"Four thousand. Maybe less if we can get a payment plan."

Penelope looked around the room. "Can we raise four thousand pounds? As a community?"

Silence. Then Mrs. Bramble stood. "I'll put in five hundred."

Maeve stood. "Two hundred from the bakery's emergency fund."

One by one, villagers stood and made pledges. Not everyone. Not huge amounts. But enough. Small contributions from dozens of people adding up to something significant.

When they finished tallying, they had four thousand, three hundred pounds.

Tom Thomas was crying. "I don't... I can't accept..."

"You're not accepting charity," Penelope said. "You're accepting help from a community that values you. That's what the threads mean, Tom. You're not alone. Your grandson isn't alone. You're part of something larger. And that's what Omni Corp wants to destroy. Not your property. Your belonging."

She turned to address the whole room. "I can't tell you not to sell. Some of you might have needs that are bigger than community can meet. But I can tell you what you'll lose. I can show you."

She opened the Sight and reached out, not to channel the Heartstone's power like she had before, but simply to share what she saw. To let a ghost of the threads become visible to everyone in the room.

It lasted only a few seconds. A glimpse. A flash of gold and silver and bronze light connecting everyone to everyone else.

But it was enough.

The room sat in stunned silence.

Finally, Mrs. Henderson spoke. Her voice shook with emotion. "I've lived in Asterly for sixty years. Raised my children here. Watched my grandchildren grow up here. And I've never... I knew we were connected. But I never saw it. Never understood how deep it went."

"That's what you're protecting," Penelope said. "Not just buildings or property values. This. Connection. Belonging. Community. The things money can't replace."

The meeting continued for another two hours. Plans were made. A community fund established to help residents with unexpected expenses, reducing vulnerability to corporate buyouts. Legal protections researched. Support networks strengthened.

When everyone finally left, Penelope collapsed on Eleanor's settee, exhausted.

Rhys sat beside her. "You did good tonight."

"I don't know if it's enough. If Omni Corp keeps increasing their offers, if they pressure people legally or financially..."

"Then we'll deal with it. Together. You're not alone in this, Penelope."

She leaned against him, feeling the dawn gold thread pulse warm between them. "What if I can't protect them? What if Omni Corp is too big, too well funded, too patient?"

"Then we fight anyway. Because the alternative is accepting that connection doesn't matter. That profit should always win over community. Eleanor spent forty three years fighting that belief. We can at least try to continue her work."

"I love you," Penelope said quietly. The words still felt new, uncertain. But true.

"I love you too." He kissed her hair. "And we're going to win this. Maybe not every battle. But the war. We're going to win the war."

Outside, in the oak grove, the Heartstone pulsed. Not a warning this time. An affirmation.

But that night, alone in Eleanor's study, Penelope faced the reality of what she was up against.

She'd spent hours researching community protection laws, land trusts, heritage designations. Every avenue seemed blocked by modern property regulations that favored developers over communities.

Eleanor's journals contained notes about community protection, dated references to 1990s legislation that had since been replaced. The Companies Act of 2006 had changed everything. The Localism Act of 2011 created new loopholes. Twenty years of corporate-friendly legal evolution had made villages like Asterly vulnerable in ways Eleanor couldn't have anticipated.

Penelope pulled up her laptop and emailed Robert Chen, her former colleague.

Robert - Need help. Community facing corporate buyout. What legal protections exist under current law? - P

His reply came an hour later:

Penelope, Not much, honestly. Community Asset listing is your best bet, but it's a bureaucratic nightmare and takes months. Land trusts can work but require majority community buy-in AND significant legal expertise to structure properly. Corporate entities have massive advantages under current competition law. You'll be fighting uphill all the way. Happy to consult but be realistic about odds. - R

She stared at the email, feeling the weight of it. This wasn't going to be easy. There was no convenient legal framework, no simple solution. Eleanor had protected Asterly through personal relationships and quiet influence, not legal structures.

If Penelope wanted to save this place, she'd have to build those protections herself, from scratch, against a well-funded opponent who knew every loophole.

The fight had truly begun. But Asterly had something Omni Corp didn't understand. Something that couldn't be quantified or purchased or developed away.

They had a Seer who could show them what they were fighting for.

And they had each other.

CHAPTER SEVEN

Marcus Thorne returned to Asterly every day for two weeks.

He was methodical, strategic, never pressuring but always present. Sitting in Mrs. Bramble's tea shop, chatting pleasantly with villagers. Touring properties with interested sellers. Making himself a familiar, non threatening presence.

It was brilliant strategy. And it was working.

Three families had accepted preliminary offers. The Carters, who wanted to retire to Spain. The Bells, who'd been struggling to maintain their farm. And worryingly, one of the Patels' cousins, who owned a cottage on the village outskirts.

Penelope met with each family, not to pressure them but to ensure they understood the implications. But she couldn't stop people from making their own choices. And the money Omni Corp offered was genuinely life changing.

On the fifteenth day of Thorne's presence, he requested a meeting with Penelope.

They met at a pub in the next village over. Neutral ground. Thorne ordered whiskey. Penelope ordered tea.

"You've been impressive, Ms. Lowell," he began. "The community fund, the legal protections, the way you've organized resistance. Most people don't fight this hard."

"Most people don't understand what they're losing."

"And you do? You've been in Asterly, what, three weeks? You're a London lawyer playing at village guardian. Don't pretend you understand this community better than the people who've lived here their whole lives."

His words stung because they had truth in them. She was an outsider. Had no right to tell lifelong residents what to value or protect.

But then she thought of Eleanor. Of the threads. Of what the Sight revealed about connection and belonging.

"You're right," she said. "I am an outsider. But I can see something the villagers can't. I can see what they're part of. What generations of their families built. What you want to destroy."

"I don't want to destroy anything. I want to develop. There's a difference."

"Is there? Show me one village Omni Corp has developed that's maintained its community. One place where local families still live, local businesses still thrive, connection still matters."

Thorne was quiet for a moment. Then he set down his whiskey. "That's not the business model."

"I know."

"The model is acquisition, development, profit. Community preservation isn't part of the equation. It can't be. Communities are messy, resistant to change, economically inefficient. Better to clear them out, start fresh, build something profitable."

"And you see nothing wrong with that?"

"I see economic reality. Villages like Asterly are dying anyway. Young people leave for cities. Industries decline. Populations age. Omni Corp just speeds up the inevitable. We give people money to start over somewhere else. How is that cruel?"

Penelope opened her Sight and looked at Thorne properly. Really looked.

There were no threads connecting him to Asterly. That was expected. But there were also remarkably few threads connecting him to anything. A thin silver line to a woman somewhere far away. His mother, perhaps. A few bronze threads to colleagues, professional relationships only. And that was all.

He was isolated. Nearly severed from the network entirely. Whether by choice or circumstance, Marcus Thorne lived in a world where connection didn't exist. Where relationships were transactional, temporary, meaningless.

No wonder he couldn't understand what he was destroying. He'd never experienced it himself.

"I'm sorry," Penelope said quietly.

He looked startled. "For what?"

"For whatever happened to you. Whatever made you think connection doesn't matter."

"Don't psychoanalyze me, Ms. Lowell. I'm here representing a business interest, not seeking therapy."

"I know. But you're wrong about Asterly dying. It's not dying. It's living. Thriving, even. The connections here are strong, healthy, growing stronger. And we're going to keep it that way."

Thorne finished his whiskey. "You can't win this fight. You know that, right? Omni Corp has purchased three properties already. We'll purchase more. Eventually, we'll have enough to claim the village center, get planning permission, force compulsory sale of the remaining properties including yours. It's just a matter of time."

"Then we'll make the time matter. Every day we delay you is a day the community grows stronger. Every connection we build is one more thread you'll have to sever. We're not going to make this easy."

"I never expected you would." He stood, left money on the table for both their drinks. "For what it's worth, I respect your commitment. But respect doesn't change outcomes. Omni Corp always wins eventually. Always."

After he left, Penelope sat in the pub for a long time, her tea growing cold.

He was right about one thing. Omni Corp had resources she couldn't match. Money, lawyers, political connections.

They could wait years if necessary. Slowly accumulating properties, building their legal case, wearing down resistance.

But they didn't have what she had.

They didn't have the Sight. Didn't have the ability to show people what mattered. Didn't have a community that understood what they were protecting.

And they didn't have Eleanor's forty three years of research. Decades of accumulated knowledge about Heartstones, about thread networks, about how connection worked.

Penelope drove back to Asterly and spent the evening in Eleanor's attic, reading through journals she hadn't examined yet. Looking for anything that might help. Any technique, any knowledge, any advantage.

She found it in a journal from 1998.

Eleanor had documented a legal strategy. Not magical, purely practical. How to establish conservation easements that would make development nearly impossible. How to use historical designation, environmental protection laws, cultural heritage status. How to build legal walls so thick that even well funded corporations would break themselves against them.

Eleanor had started implementing the strategy. Had gotten halfway through before Thomas died and she'd been forced to focus all her energy on just maintaining the Heartstone alone.

But the groundwork was there. Documented. Ready to be completed.

Penelope spent all night reading. By morning, she had a plan.

She called Rhys at dawn. "I need you to gather the village council. Today. I've found something."

They met in Sunlit Grove's dining room again. Fifteen council members, plus Rhys and Mrs. Bramble. Penelope spread Eleanor's journals and her own notes across the table.

"Eleanor started building legal protections twenty four years ago," she explained. "Conservation easements, heritage designations, environmental protections. She got most of the way through the process, but then Thomas died and she couldn't finish. But the work is still valid. The applications are still pending. We just need to complete what she started."

"How long will that take?" Tom Thomas asked.

"If I work on it full time, using my legal background and Eleanor's research? Six weeks. Maybe eight. We file for historical village designation, environmental conservation status, cultural heritage protection. Layer after layer of legal protection. And once they're in place, Omni Corp can't develop here without permission from multiple government agencies. Permission that will take years to get, if it's granted at all."

"And you can actually do this?" Mrs. Henderson asked.

"I can. I spent ten years as a corporate lawyer. I know how to navigate planning regulations, how to file applications, how to build ironclad legal cases. This is what I'm good at."

"But you said it'll take weeks. What if Omni Corp purchases more properties in the meantime?"

"Then we need to slow them down. Make every potential seller understand what's at stake. Give them reasons to wait, to resist, to hold out just a little longer while I build the legal protections."

The council debated for hours. Some wanted to trust Penelope's plan. Others worried it was too slow, too uncertain. But eventually, consensus emerged.

They would fight. On multiple fronts. Legal protections, community organizing, direct resistance. Everything they had.

As the meeting broke up, Rhys pulled Penelope aside. "This is brilliant. Eleanor's work, your legal expertise. This could actually stop them."

"If we're fast enough. If Omni Corp doesn't outmaneuver us. If I don't make any legal mistakes." She rubbed her eyes, exhausted from the all night research session. "There are a lot of if's, Rhys."

"Then we'd better make them all work in our favor."

Over the next six weeks, Penelope lived in Eleanor's study. Surrounded by legal documents, planning regulations, heritage applications. She used every skill she'd developed in corporate law, every contact she'd maintained, every favor she could call in.

And she discovered something surprising. Eleanor had been building more than just legal protections. She'd been building a network.

Correspondence with other guardians. Other villages with Heartstones. Sites across the UK facing similar threats. Eleanor had documented them all, had reached out, had tried to build solidarity.

Most hadn't responded. But some had. A guardian in Wales. One in Scotland. Another in Cornwall. Small notes of support, sharing of strategies, acknowledgment that they were fighting the same battle.

Eleanor had been trying to do what Penelope was now attempting. Connect the isolated guardians. Build a network that could resist together instead of falling one by one.

She'd just run out of time.

But Penelope had time. Had the legal skills Eleanor lacked. Had Rhys as a partner instead of fighting mostly alone. Had a village that understood what they were protecting.

She could finish what Eleanor started.

Both the legal protections and the network of guardians.

On a cold November morning, eight weeks after Marcus Thorne first arrived in Asterly, Penelope filed the final applications. Historical village designation. Environmental conservation status. Cultural heritage protection. Everything Eleanor had planned, now complete and submitted.

The applications would take months to process. But once filed, they created legal limbo. Development couldn't proceed while heritage status was being considered. Omni Corp couldn't force sales while conservation applications were pending.

They'd bought time. Months, maybe a year. Long enough to strengthen the community, build resistance, make Asterly too costly to attack.

Marcus Thorne left the village three days later. His car driving away without ceremony or threat. Just quiet retreat.

But Penelope knew he'd be back. Omni Corp didn't give up just because one strategy failed. They'd try another approach. Legal challenges, political pressure, something.

The fight wasn't over.

It was only beginning.

But Asterly had survived the first assault. And they were stronger for it.

That night, she and Rhys stood in the oak grove. The Heartstone glowed contentedly, its threads stable and strong. The village had rallied, had fought, had protected what mattered.

"Eleanor would be proud," Rhys said.

"Eleanor did most of the work. I just finished what she started."

"You did more than that. You united the village. Showed them what they're protecting. Gave them tools to fight. That's not just finishing Eleanor's work. That's continuing it. Building on it."

Penelope touched the Heartstone, felt its warmth through her palm. Eight weeks ago, she'd been a London lawyer who didn't believe in magic. Now she was a guardian, a Seer, someone who fought to protect connection itself.

The transformation was complete.

She was home.

CHAPTER EIGHT

Two weeks back in Asterly, and Penelope had stopped thinking of London entirely.

The October mornings were crisp now, mist rising from the wild garden in silver tendrils that caught the early light. She'd fallen into a rhythm with Rhys. He arrived at nine every morning with coffee and whatever pastries Maeve had baked that day, and they worked until sunset, pausing only when Penelope's head began to throb from extended use of the Sight.

Today they sat in Eleanor's study, the one room Penelope had claimed as truly hers. She'd moved Eleanor's research to the attic and brought down her own books. Legal texts mixed with the grimoires and journals Eleanor had left behind, an odd marriage of two worlds that somehow made sense now.

"Focus on the Harrison house," Rhys said, watching her from the leather armchair. "See if you can sense the family bonds without getting pulled into them."

Penelope closed her eyes and opened the Sight. Immediately, the world exploded into color. Threads everywhere. Gold and silver and bronze and crimson, weaving through the village like an impossibly complex spider's web. She could see every connection: Mrs. Bramble's silver thread to her tea shop, the Patels' crimson family bonds stretching back generations, Maeve's golden thread to every person she'd ever fed.

It was overwhelming. Beautiful and terrible and so much more than human eyes were meant to perceive.

She forced herself to narrow focus, to see only what she was looking for. The Harrison house, on the north edge of the village square. There, she found the threads connecting the family. Mr. Harrison's bronze thread to his wife, forty-seven years strong. Their children's crimson bonds, healthy and bright. And underneath, something she hadn't expected: a frayed silver thread connecting Mr. Harrison to his brother in Manchester, almost severed completely.

"There's damage," she said aloud, her eyes still closed. "Harrison and his brother. The thread's barely holding."

"Good. You're seeing clearly. Now, can you tell me why without getting lost in it?"

She pushed her perception deeper, following the damaged thread, and immediately felt herself being pulled into it. Emotions flooded through her. Anger, betrayal, grief. A disagreement over their father's will, harsh words spoken years ago and never taken back, pride preventing reconciliation.

"Penelope." Rhys's voice, sharp. "Come back."

She tried. But the emotions were so strong, and she was being pulled deeper into the story, losing track of where she ended and the thread began.

Warm hands gripped her shoulders. The dawn-gold thread between her and Rhys flared brilliant, and suddenly she could feel him through it. His steadiness, his certainty, his absolute conviction that she was Penelope Lowell and not a collection of someone else's memories and emotions.

She gasped and opened her eyes.

Rhys was kneeling beside her chair, his hands still on her shoulders, his grey eyes locked on hers. "You went too deep."

"I know. I'm sorry, I just... the emotions were so strong, and I wanted to understand why the thread broke, and..."

"That's the danger." He released her shoulders but stayed close. "The Sight shows you everything. Every connection, every emotion, every memory that's woven into the threads. If you're not careful, you start experiencing them like they're your own. You lose yourself."

Penelope's hands were shaking. "How do you do it? How do you pull me back?"

"The Guardian bond." He settled back on his heels, his expression serious. "I can sense when you're too deep because our thread connects us. When I feel you slipping, I can... reach through it. Remind you of yourself. Of who you are apart from what you're Seeing."

"And if you weren't here?"

"You'd eventually find your way back. Probably. But you'd be lost for hours, maybe days. My grandfather told me about Seers who got permanently tangled in the network. Spent the rest of their lives unable to distinguish their own emotions from everyone else's."

A chill ran down her spine. "That's horrifying."

"That's why Seers need Guardians." Rhys stood, moving back to his chair. "You're getting better at controlling the Sight, but you're also getting deeper into it. Which means the risks are increasing."

"So what do I do? Stop using it?"

"No. You learn to trust the bond. To let me anchor you when you go too deep." He paused. "Which means we need to strengthen the connection between us. Make it automatic, instinctive. So I can pull you back even when you're not aware you're lost."

"How do we do that?"

His expression shifted. Uncertain, almost vulnerable. "Physical contact helps. The more we're actually touching when you use the Sight, the stronger the anchor becomes."

"Physical contact." Penelope felt heat rise to her cheeks. "Like... holding hands?"

"Or sitting closer. Or, yes, like holding hands." He looked away. "It's not romantic, before you think that. It's practical. The bond works through touch."

"I didn't say it was romantic."

"You were thinking it."

"I was not..." She stopped, because she absolutely had been thinking it. The memory of his hands on her shoulders was still warm on her skin, and the dawn-gold thread between them was pulsing with something that felt decidedly less than professional.

Rhys seemed to be having the same realization, because he cleared his throat and stood abruptly. "Right. Well. We should practice that. The touching. For anchoring purposes."

"Right. Anchoring purposes."

"Purely practical."

"Absolutely."

They stared at each other for a beat too long.

The knock at the door made them both jump.

Mrs. Bramble's voice called from outside: "Penelope, dear? I've brought lunch. And news."

Penelope opened the door to find Mrs. Bramble carrying a basket and wearing an expression of deep concern. Behind her, Maeve hovered nervously.

"What's wrong?" Penelope asked immediately.

"The Thomases," Mrs. Bramble said, setting the basket on the entrance hall table. "Omni Corp approached them yesterday. Made an offer. A serious one."

"How serious?"

"Nine hundred thousand pounds for their hardware shop and the flat above it." Maeve's voice was tight. "The property's worth maybe three hundred and fifty thousand. It's a fortune, Penelope. And Tom Thomas has a grandson who needs expensive medical treatment. The kind the NHS won't fully cover."

Penelope's stomach sank. "They're considering it."

"They're more than considering it," Mrs. Bramble said gently. "They're meeting with Omni Corp's lawyers today to discuss terms."

Rhys swore under his breath. "If the Thomases sell, Omni Corp has a property right on the village square. They can argue historical significance, get planning permission for wider development."

"Can we stop them?" Maeve asked, looking between Penelope and Rhys desperately. "Legally? Magically? Something?"

Penelope thought fast, her lawyer's mind engaging. "Legally, no. It's their property. They can sell if they want. But..." She looked at Rhys. "Could we show them? What they'd be losing? The way you showed me the threads in the garden that first day?"

"You want to share your Sight with them."

"If they could see what I see, the generations of threads connecting their family to this place, the web of relationships they're part of, maybe they'd understand what money can't replace."

"That's dangerous," Rhys warned. "Sharing the Sight takes enormous energy. Eleanor did it once with a single person and was bedridden for three days."

"But it's possible?"

"With a Guardian to anchor you, yes. But Penelope..."

"We have to try." She turned to Mrs. Bramble. "Can you arrange a meeting? At Sunlit Grove, this evening. The Thomases and anyone else who's been approached by Omni Corp. Tell them I want to show them something."

Mrs. Bramble's eyes widened. "You're going to make them See."

"You know about...?"

"Dear, everyone knows Eleanor could do things normal people couldn't. We just didn't talk about it. Made her uncomfortable." She smiled. "But yes, I'll arrange it. Seven o'clock?"

"Seven o'clock," Penelope confirmed.

After the women left, Rhys rounded on her. "Do you understand what you're committing to? Sharing the Sight with multiple people simultaneously? That's not like mending a single heartline. That's channeling the entire network through yourself and projecting it outward. It could kill you."

"Then you'll anchor me and make sure it doesn't."

"Penelope..."

"We're out of options, Rhys. We can't fight Omni Corp with lawyers and petitions alone. They have too much money, too many connections. But we have something they don't. We can show people the truth. The actual, visible truth about what they're protecting." She moved closer to him, close enough to feel the warmth radiating from his body. "You said the bond between us needs to be stronger. That touch makes it stronger. So let's make it strong enough to do this."

He stared at her, conflict clear in his grey eyes. Then, slowly, he extended his hand. "If we're doing this, we do it properly. All day, until the meeting. Building the connection until it's second nature."

Penelope took his hand. The moment their palms touched, the dawn-gold thread between them blazed so bright it was almost painful. She gasped as sensation flooded through the connection. His fear for her safety, his determination to protect her, his bone-deep certainty that she was the right person for this burden, and underneath it all, something warmer and more complex that neither of them were quite ready to name.

"All day," she agreed, her voice barely above a whisper.

They spent the afternoon learning each other through the thread. Sitting close on Eleanor's settee, hands clasped, letting the bond deepen until Penelope could sense Rhys's heartbeat like it was her own. Until his steady presence became a constant hum in the back of her consciousness, grounding her even when she wasn't actively using the Sight.

It was intimate in a way that had nothing to do with romance and everything to do with trust. She learned the texture of his thoughts, the pattern of his breathing, the way his mind worked when he was focused. And he learned her. The sharp edges of her analytical thinking, the vulnerability she hid beneath professional competence, the fear that she wasn't enough to carry Eleanor's legacy.

"You are enough," he said at one point, apparently sensing the doubt through their connection.

"How do you know?"

"Because Eleanor chose you. And because the Heartstone accepted you. Neither of those things happen by accident."

By the time seven o'clock arrived, the bond between them had transformed. No longer tentative or uncertain, it was a solid bridge. Strong enough, she hoped, to keep her tethered while she did something Eleanor had considered too dangerous to attempt more than once.

The parlor of Sunlit Grove filled with villagers as evening darkened to night. The Thomases, looking worried and guilty. The Patels, the Harrisons, the elderly Mrs. Henderson who ran the post office. Mrs. Bramble and Maeve, serving tea and providing moral support. Fifteen people in total, all of whom had been approached by Omni Corp, all of whom were wavering.

Penelope stood at the front of the room, Rhys beside her, and felt the weight of their expectations pressing down like a physical force.

"Thank you for coming," she began, her voice steadier than she felt. "I know Omni Corp has made you generous offers. Life-changing amounts of money. And I'm not here to tell you that money doesn't matter. I know some of you have needs. Medical bills, education costs, retirement funds."

She saw Tom Thomas flinch and knew she'd hit home.

"But I want to show you something before you make your final decisions. Something my great-aunt Eleanor could see, and something I've inherited from her. The connections that make Asterly what it is. Not metaphorical connections. Real, visible threads of light that bind this community together."

Murmurs rippled through the crowd. Skeptical looks, concerned glances.

"I know how it sounds," Penelope continued. "Believe me, I know. Two weeks ago, I would have called myself insane for saying this. But I'm going to prove it to you. For the next few minutes, I'm going to share my Sight with you. You'll see what I see. And then you can make your decisions with full knowledge of what you're protecting."

She turned to Rhys. "Ready?"

"Ready." He took both her hands, and the dawn-gold thread between them pulsed with power. "Remember, I've got you. No matter how deep you go, I'll pull you back."

"I know." And she did know. Could feel his certainty through the bond like it was her own.

Penelope opened the Sight fully. The room exploded into light. Threads everywhere, connecting everyone to everyone else. Silver threads of friendship, bronze threads of shared history, crimson threads of family bonds stretching back generations. And beneath it all, gold threads connecting each person to Asterly itself, to the land and the buildings and the accumulated weight of centuries.

Beautiful. Overwhelming. Impossible.

Now came the hard part.

She reached out, not with her hands but with her will, her intention, and grasped the network. Pulled it toward herself, let it flow through her like water through a sieve. Every connection, every emotion, every memory woven into the threads. It was agony. Ecstasy. Too much, far too much for one person to contain.

Through the pain, she heard Rhys's voice: "I've got you. Stay with me."

The dawn-gold thread between them became her lifeline. She clung to it, let it remind her that she was Penelope Lowell, that she had an identity apart from the network, that she wouldn't be consumed by what she was channeling.

And then she pushed outward.

The threads blazed visible to everyone in the room.

Someone screamed. Someone else gasped. But then, silence.

Because they were all Seeing it now. The web of connections that made them a community. Mrs. Henderson's thread to the post office, forty-three years of service woven into silver light. The Patels' crimson family bonds, seven generations of ancestors watching over them through threads that glowed like embers. Tom Thomas's bronze thread to his hardware shop, and beneath it, the golden thread connecting his grandson to the entire village. Every person who'd donated to the medical fund, every shopkeeper who'd given the family discounts, every neighbor who'd brought meals during the worst days.

Penelope held it for three minutes. Three minutes of showing them what Omni Corp wanted to destroy. What no amount of money could replace.

Then she released it.

The threads vanished from common view, and Penelope collapsed.

Rhys caught her before she hit the floor, his arms solid and warm around her. "I've got you," he murmured. "You did it. Now come back."

The world spun. She was tangled in the network, lost in the maze of connections, unable to find her own thread among the thousands.

The dawn-gold bond flared brilliant. Rhys, pulling her back. Reminding her of herself.

She gasped and opened her eyes.

The parlor was silent. Every villager sat frozen, tears streaming down faces, expressions of wonder and grief and understanding.

Tom Thomas spoke first, his voice rough. "That was... we're all..."

"Connected," Penelope finished weakly. "You're all part of something bigger than property values and profit margins. Omni Corp can't offer you that. They can offer money. But they can't offer you belonging."

"I'm not selling," Tom said firmly. "I don't care how much they offer. I'm not severing those threads. I'm not destroying what I just saw."

Murmurs of agreement rippled through the room.

One by one, the villagers stood and made their commitments. Not selling. Fighting together. Protecting what mattered.

When the room finally emptied, leaving only Rhys and Penelope in the aftermath, she was shaking with exhaustion. Every muscle ached. Her head throbbed. But they'd won. For tonight, at least, they'd won.

"You need to rest," Rhys said, guiding her toward the stairs.

"I'm fine."

"You're not fine. You channeled the entire village's thread network through yourself for three minutes. That's not fine." He stopped at the base of the stairs. "Let me help you up."

"Rhys, I can walk."

"I know you can. But you don't have to." He held out his hand. "Let me help."

She took his hand, and together they climbed the stairs to the bedroom she'd claimed as hers. The one that overlooked the wild garden and the woods beyond.

"Will you stay?" she asked, suddenly terrified of being alone. Of losing herself again in the threads without his anchor.

"Of course." He settled into the chair by the window, the same chair Eleanor must have sat in hundreds of times. "Sleep. I'll be here."

"Promise?"

"Promise."

Penelope fell asleep with the dawn-gold thread humming between them, Rhys's steady presence a constant reassurance that she was herself, that she was safe, that she wasn't alone in this impossible responsibility.

Outside, in the oak grove beyond the wild garden, the Heartstone pulsed once. Approving.

CHAPTER NINE

Penelope woke to grey morning light and the smell of coffee.

She sat up, disoriented, and found Rhys still in the chair by the window, a takeaway cup in his hand and dark circles under his eyes.

"Did you sleep at all?" she asked, her voice raspy.

"A bit." He handed her the second cup he'd brought. "How do you feel?"

"Like I was hit by a lorry." She took the coffee gratefully. "But alive. That counts for something."

"You were brilliant last night. I've never seen anything like it. Eleanor used to share the Sight with one person at a time, and even that exhausted her. You showed fifteen people simultaneously and held it for three full minutes."

"Only because you anchored me." She met his eyes over the rim of her cup. "I would have been lost without you."

Something passed between them. Understanding, perhaps. Or acknowledgment of how deeply they'd become entangled in each other's lives. The dawn-gold thread pulsed with warmth.

Rhys cleared his throat and stood. "Mrs. Bramble will be by with breakfast soon. And I suspect the village council will want to meet. Last night changed things. People are committed now in a way they weren't before."

"Omni Corp won't give up."

"No. But they'll have a much harder fight on their hands." He moved toward the door, then paused. "Penelope? Thank you. For doing this. For staying. Eleanor would be proud."

After he left, Penelope showered and dressed, trying to reclaim some sense of normalcy. But nothing felt normal anymore. She could still feel the echo of last night's working, the ghost of fifteen people's threads flowing through her consciousness. It was disorienting and wonderful and terrifying all at once.

By the time she made it downstairs, Mrs. Bramble had indeed arrived, and had taken over the kitchen with the ease of someone who'd done this many times before.

"Eleanor always needed feeding after a major working," the older woman said, setting out eggs and bacon and toast with ruthless efficiency. "You look like you need it even more. Sit. Eat."

Penelope sat and ate, grateful for someone else taking charge.

"The whole village is talking about what you did," Mrs. Bramble continued, pouring tea. "Tom Thomas has been telling everyone. About the threads, about seeing his grandson's connection to the community. Half the people think it's a miracle. The other half think it's witchcraft."

"And you?"

Mrs. Bramble smiled. "I think it's what Eleanor always wanted. For people to truly see what they have here. What's worth protecting." She sobered. "But Marcus Thorne was in the village this morning. He didn't look happy."

"He wouldn't be. We just cost him a significant property acquisition."

"Be careful, dear. Men like that don't take kindly to being thwarted."

As if summoned by the mention of his name, there was a sharp knock at the door. Penelope opened it to find Marcus Thorne standing on the step, his expensive suit immaculate, his smile fixed and cold.

"Ms. Lowell. May I come in?"

"No."

"I think you'll want to hear what I have to say."

"I don't care what you have to say. You're not welcome on my property."

His smile didn't waver. "I'm sure whatever... performance you put on last night was very impressive. But tricks and parlor games won't change the economic realities. Asterly is dying. Young people are leaving. Businesses are struggling. We're offering a lifeline."

"You're offering destruction dressed up as opportunity. And the village has made their choice."

"For now." He pulled out his phone, showed her a photograph. The oak grove. The Heartstone clearly visible in the image. "We know what you have, Ms. Lowell. We know what this property really is. And we know that sites like this exist elsewhere. Your little village isn't unique. It's just... unusually stubborn."

Ice flooded Penelope's veins. "How long have you known?"

"About the Heartstone? Years. We've been monitoring Eleanor Lowell for quite some time. Waiting for the property to change hands. Hoping for a more... reasonable heir."

"Get off my property."

"I'll go. But understand this: Omni Corp doesn't lose. We've acquired seventeen similar sites across the UK. All of them had guardians like you. All of them had communities that resisted. And all of them eventually sold. Because we're patient. Because we're well-funded. And because, in the end, everyone has a price."

"Not everyone."

"We'll see." He pocketed his phone. "Oh, and Ms. Lowell? You might want to check on the Heartstone in the oak grove. It looked... stressed when we photographed it yesterday. Something about electromagnetic equipment interfering with its frequency. Fascinating phenomenon, really."

He walked away before she could respond.

Penelope stood frozen in the doorway, fury and fear warring in her chest.

Mrs. Bramble appeared beside her. "What did he say?"

"He knows about the Heartstone. They've been monitoring it. And they did something to it yesterday. Interfered with it somehow." She grabbed her coat. "I need to check on it. Now."

Rhys appeared as if summoned, and together they ran through the wild garden toward the woods. The path to the oak grove felt longer than usual, every step weighted with dread.

They burst into the clearing and stopped.

The Heartstone was dimmer than it should be. Its usual pearl-like glow had faded to a sickly grey. And the threads radiating from it, usually vibrant and strong, were flickering like dying embers.

"No," Penelope whispered.

Rhys moved closer, his expression grim. "They've damaged it somehow. Weakened it."

"Can we fix it?"

"I don't know. I've never seen damage like this." He turned to her. "You need to try. Use the Sight. See if you can sense what's wrong."

Penelope opened the Sight and immediately gasped. The Heartstone's threads weren't just dim. They were fraying. Hundreds of connections, slowly unraveling. As if something had attacked the very fabric of the network.

"It's coming apart," she said, horror in her voice. "The threads are breaking. All of them."

"Can you mend them?"

"There are too many. Dozens, hundreds. I can't..."

"Yes, you can." Rhys took her hand. "You mended the Patels' thread. You mended the Harrisons' thread. This is the same thing, just larger scale."

"This isn't the same. This is the entire village's thread network. If I try to channel that much, it'll kill me."

"Not if I'm anchoring you. Not if we do it together." He squeezed her hand. "I trust you, Penelope. And you need to trust me. Trust the bond. Trust that I won't let you get lost."

She looked at the dying Heartstone, then at Rhys. His grey eyes were steady, certain. The dawn-gold thread between them pulsed with strength.

"All right," she said quietly. "Let's try."

They knelt beside the Heartstone, hands clasped, and Penelope opened the Sight fully. The damage was worse up close. Threads snapping and reforming and snapping again, a chaos of light and dissolution. She reached out with her will and grasped the first broken thread.

Pain lanced through her. The thread fought her, tried to pull her into its unraveling. But Rhys was there, steady and strong through their bond, reminding her of herself.

She held on. Forced the thread to remember its purpose, its connection. Wove the frayed ends back together.

One thread mended.

Six hundred and forty-three to go.

She lost track of time. Lost track of everything except the threads and Rhys's presence. One by one, she mended the breaks. Reinforced the weak points. Poured her will and her strength into rebuilding what Omni Corp had tried to destroy.

Hours passed. The sun moved across the sky. Her head throbbed. Her hands shook. But she kept working.

And Rhys kept her anchored. Every time she started to slip, every time the network threatened to consume her, he pulled her back. His voice, his presence, the solid certainty of the dawn-gold thread reminding her that she was Penelope Lowell and not just a conduit for the Tethering Light.

Finally, as the sun began to set, she wove the last thread back into place.

The Heartstone blazed brilliant. Brighter than before. Every thread glowing strong and healthy.

Penelope collapsed into Rhys's arms, completely spent.

"You did it," he murmured into her hair. "Every thread. You saved them all."

"We did it," she corrected weakly. "I would have been lost without you."

He held her close, and she could feel his heart hammering against her cheek. They'd done something impossible today. Something Eleanor had never attempted. Mended an entire village's worth of threads in a single working.

And Omni Corp would know about it. Would know they'd failed.

"They'll try again," Penelope said.

"I know. But we'll be ready. And next time, the whole village will be ready too."

They sat in the oak grove as twilight deepened, the Heartstone pulsing contentedly, and Penelope understood something fundamental. This was her life now. Not contracts and mergers and boardroom negotiations. But threads and magic and fighting to protect connections that most people couldn't even see.

And despite the exhaustion, despite the danger, despite upending everything she'd worked a decade to build, she wouldn't change it.

Because for the first time in her life, she was doing something that mattered. Really mattered.

"Thank you," she said quietly to Rhys.

"For what?"

"For believing I could do this. For anchoring me. For..." She hesitated. "For being here."

"There's nowhere else I'd rather be." He said it simply, like stating a fact. But through the dawn-gold thread, she felt the depth of truth behind his words.

They walked back to Sunlit Grove as stars began to appear overhead. And Penelope felt the first stirrings of something beyond partnership, beyond the Guardian bond.

Something warmer. Something more dangerous.

Something she wasn't quite ready to name.

CHAPTER TEN

Three days after mending the Heartstone, Penelope received an email from her former firm.

She'd been avoiding checking her London email, but curiosity got the better of her. The message was from Robert, her old senior partner:

Penelope,

Omni Corp has retained our firm for a major development project in the Cotswolds. They specifically requested that we NOT involve you due to conflict of interest. I'm respecting your resignation, but I thought you should know: they're serious about Asterly. Very serious. Whatever you did to stop their property acquisitions has only made them more determined.

Be careful.

Robert

She showed the email to Rhys over morning coffee.

"They're escalating," he said, his expression grim.

"I know. But I don't understand their endgame. Why is Omni Corp so determined to destroy the Heartstone? What do they gain from severing the thread network?"

"That's what we need to find out." Rhys pulled out his laptop. A surprising sight, given his preference for old books and analog research. "I've been digging into Omni Corp's corporate structure. And it gets strange."

He turned the screen toward her. A maze of subsidiary companies, shell corporations, and holding companies, all ultimately tracing back to a parent organization called Severance Holdings.

"Severance," Penelope murmured. "Ironic name for a company targeting connection sites."

"It's more than ironic. Look at their other holdings." He clicked through several screens. Development companies, yes, but also telecommunications firms, social media platforms, logistics companies. All businesses that, on the surface, claimed to connect people but in practice seemed designed to isolate them.

"They're systematically destroying organic connections and replacing them with artificial ones," Penelope said slowly. "Ones they control."

"That's my theory. And if you look at where they've successfully developed in the past..." He pulled up a map. Red pins marked seventeen locations across the UK. "These were all villages with Heartstones or similar connection sites. After Omni Corp developed them, the communities fragmented. Young people moved away faster than before. Local businesses failed. Within ten years, each village became essentially a commuter suburb with no real identity."

Penelope studied the map, her legal mind processing the pattern. "They're not just building developments. They're conducting a systematic campaign against community itself."

"But why? What's the motivation?"

"Profit, maybe. Isolated people consume more, save less, make purchasing decisions based on advertising rather than community recommendations." She paused. "Or it's ideological. Some people genuinely believe that traditional communities are obstacles to progress. That we'd all be better off as atomized individuals making rational economic choices."

"That's horrifying."

"That's late-stage capitalism." She closed the laptop. "But whatever their motivation, they've made a mistake. They assumed I'd be like their other targets. Someone they could buy off or intimidate. They didn't count on me having you. On us having the village behind us."

"So what do we do?"

Penelope smiled. It wasn't a pleasant smile. It was the smile she'd worn in high-stakes negotiations back in London. The smile that meant someone was about to lose and lose badly.

"We go on the offensive. I'm a lawyer, Rhys. I know how corporations work. How they think. And I know their weak points." She stood, pacing. "Omni Corp has been operating in the shadows, targeting rural villages that don't have resources to fight back. But what if we make this public? What if we expose their pattern?"

"The Heartstones are real. You can't expose them without revealing magic."

"I don't need to mention the Heartstones specifically. I just need to document the pattern. Seventeen villages, all developed by Omni Corp, all showing the same community decline afterward. That's compelling even without mentioning thread networks." She was warming to the idea now, her mind racing ahead. "And if I can find even one legal violation in their past projects, one environmental regulation they skirted, one community consultation they didn't properly conduct, I can tie them up in court for years."

"You want to fight them with paperwork."

"I want to fight them with everything we have. Magic and law. Community resistance and legal injunctions. Make them spend money and time and political capital. Force them to decide if Asterly is worth the fight."

Rhys's expression shifted to something like admiration. "You're terrifying when you're like this. You know that, right?"

"I spent ten years learning to terrify corporate opponents. Might as well use those skills for good now." She pulled out her phone. "I need to make some calls. I still have contacts at environmental organizations, community rights groups, investigative journalists. If Omni Corp wants a fight, they're about to get one they didn't expect."

She spent the rest of the morning on the phone, reconnecting with old colleagues, explaining the situation without mentioning the magical elements. By lunchtime, she had commitments from three environmental groups to investigate Omni Corp's past projects, a journalist interested in the story, and a community rights lawyer willing to consult pro bono.

Rhys watched her work with something like awe. "You're building an army."

"I'm building a defense. There's a difference." She made another note. "But yes, essentially. Omni Corp thought they were targeting an isolated village. They're about to discover they've targeted a village with connections. Real ones. The kind that matter."

That afternoon, Mrs. Bramble arrived with news. The village council had called an emergency meeting. Several members had received phone calls from London-based firms, offering to buy their properties at extremely generous prices.

"How generous?" Penelope asked.

"Enough to retire on. Enough to never work again." Mrs. Bramble's expression was worried. "And Penelope, some of them are considering it. The Hendersons are seventy-three. They've been talking about retiring anyway. This would let them move closer to their daughter in Brighton."

"I can't blame them for that. Everyone has the right to make their own choices."

"But if enough people sell, Omni Corp won't need compulsory purchase orders. They'll just have the land."

Penelope thought for a moment. "What if we created an alternative? A way for people like the Hendersons to retire comfortably without selling to Omni Corp?"

"How would that work?"

"Community land trust. We form a legal entity, funded by the village collectively. When someone wants to sell, the trust has first right of refusal and can match the offer. That way the property stays within the community's control."

"Can that really work?"

"It's worked in other places. Hebden Bridge, Totnes, several villages in Scotland. It requires everyone to contribute, but it's a way to protect the community without forcing individuals to sacrifice their financial security."

Rhys, who'd been listening quietly, spoke up. "Eleanor had money set aside. Quite a bit, actually. She left it in trust for maintenance of the Heartstone and Grove. Could that fund be used?"

"If the trust documents are written correctly, yes." Penelope's mind was already racing ahead. "I'd need to review Eleanor's will again, see what flexibility exists. But if we can use even part of that money to establish a community land trust, we can counter Omni Corp's strategy."

Mrs. Bramble smiled. "Eleanor would approve. She always said the Heartstone wasn't just a magical object. It was a symbol of everything worth protecting. Using her legacy to protect the actual community, not just the mystical aspects, that's exactly what she would have wanted."

That evening, Penelope presented the idea to the village council. Fifteen people crammed into Mrs. Bramble's tea shop, listening intently as she explained the concept of a community land trust, showed them examples from other villages, outlined how Eleanor's estate could provide seed funding.

"It's not a perfect solution," she admitted. "You'd all have to contribute something. Pay into the trust to keep it solvent. But it means that when the Hendersons want to retire, they can sell their property at fair market value and the trust can buy it. Keep it within community control. Rent it to a young family or another shopkeeper. Preserve the continuity."

"And if Omni Corp offers more than fair market value?" someone asked.

"Then the trust will have to match it. Which is why everyone needs to contribute. This only works if the whole community commits to it."

Debate raged for two hours. Some villagers loved the idea. Others worried about the financial commitment. A few were openly skeptical that it could work.

Finally, Tom Thomas stood. "I'll contribute. I was willing to sell three days ago. But after what Penelope showed us, after seeing those threads connecting my grandson to all of you, I understand what we'd lose. I'll put in five thousand pounds to start."

One by one, other villagers made commitments. Not everyone, but enough. By the end of the evening, they had pledges for forty-three thousand pounds. Combined with Eleanor's trust fund, it was enough to establish a community land trust with real purchasing power.

Penelope felt something shift in the room. These weren't just individual property owners anymore. They were a collective. A community in the deepest sense, committed to protecting each other and their shared identity.

The threads in the room glowed brighter. She could See them even without trying, the bonds strengthening in real time as commitments were made.

After the meeting, walking back to Sunlit Grove with Rhys, she felt cautiously hopeful for the first time in days.

"You did good tonight," Rhys said. "Using both kinds of power. The legal and the magical."

"We're going to need both. Omni Corp isn't going to give up just because we've formed a land trust."

"No. But now they know they're not fighting just you. They're fighting the entire village. That changes the calculation."

They reached the Grove's gates and stopped. The evening was cool, stars beginning to appear overhead. The wild garden rustled with night sounds.

"Rhys," Penelope said quietly. "Thank you. For believing this could work. For supporting me even when I'm trying to fight corporate lawyers with mystical thread magic and community organizing."

"There's nowhere else I'd rather be." He said it simply, but through the dawn-gold thread, she felt the depth of truth behind the words.

They stood close, not quite touching but aware of the small space between them. The thread hummed with possibility.

Penelope took a breath, about to say something, about to acknowledge what had been building between them for weeks.

But a sharp pulse from the Heartstone interrupted them. A warning, urgent and clear.

Something was wrong.

They ran together through the garden toward the oak grove, and Penelope felt dread pooling in her stomach. If Omni Corp had tried to damage the Heartstone again...

But when they burst into the clearing, the Heartstone was intact. Glowing strongly. Undamaged.

And yet, something was different. The threads radiating from it had changed. One in particular, stretching out toward the horizon, pulsed with a color Penelope had never seen before.

Deep, celestial blue. Brilliant and desperate.

"What is that?" she whispered.

Rhys moved closer, his expression awed. "I don't know. I've never seen a blue thread before."

Penelope opened the Sight fully and gasped. The blue thread wasn't local. It stretched beyond the village, beyond the region, far into the distance. Hundreds of miles, perhaps. Connecting the Heartstone to something else. Something calling for help.

"There's another Heartstone," she said, understanding dawning. "Somewhere far away. And it's in trouble."

Through the blue thread, she could sense desperation. Fear. A plea for aid from someone like her, another Seer, another guardian struggling against forces they couldn't fight alone.

"The Tethering Light is bigger than just Asterly," Rhys said quietly. "My grandfather used to say that. Used to talk about a global network of Heartstones, all connected. I thought it was just theory."

"It's not theory. It's real. And someone out there needs help."

They stared at the blue thread, at the impossible distance it spanned, and Penelope understood that protecting Asterly was only the beginning. If Omni Corp was targeting Heartstone sites globally, if the pattern of severing connections was worldwide, then the fight was bigger than one village.

Bigger than anything she'd imagined.

"We have to go," she said. "Whoever that is, wherever they are, we have to help them."

"Penelope, we can't leave. Asterly needs us."

"Asterly has the land trust now. Has the village council committed to fighting. They'll hold the line while we're gone. But whoever is at the other end of that thread..." She touched the blue strand, felt the desperation pulsing through it. "They don't have anyone. They're fighting alone. The way Eleanor did after your grandfather died. I won't abandon them to that."

Rhys was quiet for a long moment. Then he nodded. "We'll need to prepare. Make sure the village can function without us. Train someone else to maintain the Heartstone's basic functions."

"How long will that take?"

"A week. Maybe two."

"Then we have two weeks to get ready. Because after that, we're following the blue thread wherever it leads."

They walked back to the Grove in silence, both processing what this meant. They'd thought the fight was contained to Asterly, to protecting one village from one corporation. But the blue thread proved otherwise.

The fight was global. And they'd just committed to joining it.

In the oak grove behind them, the Heartstone pulsed with approval. The blue thread grew slightly brighter, as if sensing that help was coming.

Somewhere, hundreds of miles away, another Seer felt the answering pulse and allowed themselves a moment of desperate hope.

CHAPTER ELEVEN

The next two weeks were a blur of preparation and training.

Penelope worked with the village council to formalize the community land trust, filing the paperwork, setting up the bank accounts, ensuring that Asterly would have legal protection in her absence. Mrs. Bramble proved surprisingly adept at organizational management, taking over coordination of the trust's operations with military efficiency.

Meanwhile, Rhys trained a young woman named Sarah Mitchell to serve as temporary guardian of the Heartstone. Sarah was twenty-three, had grown up in Asterly, and had what Rhys described as "sensitivity" to the threads. She couldn't See them the way Penelope could, but she could sense when they were healthy or damaged.

"It's not ideal," Rhys admitted after one training session. "She's not a true Seer. But she can monitor the Heartstone's basic functions. Alert the village council if something goes wrong."

"And if Omni Corp attacks while we're gone?"

"Then the village fights back. They're prepared now. They understand what they're protecting."

On the twelfth day of preparation, Marcus Thorne returned to Asterly.

Penelope was in the tea shop, finalizing trust documents with Mrs. Bramble, when he walked in. His expensive suit was as immaculate as always, but his expression was harder than before. Less charm, more threat.

"Ms. Lowell. I thought we should have a conversation."

"We have nothing to discuss."

"Oh, I think we do." He pulled out a chair uninvited and sat. "You've been very busy. Community land trusts, environmental investigations, journalists asking uncomfortable questions about our past projects. Quite impressive, really."

"Thank you."

"It wasn't a compliment." His smile was sharp. "You're making this more difficult than it needs to be. Omni Corp is willing to be generous, but our patience has limits."

"Then I suggest you take your limits elsewhere. Asterly isn't interested."

"Asterly doesn't get to decide much longer." He leaned forward. "We're filing for compulsory purchase next week. We have a judge who's sympathetic to economic development. We have local MPs who owe us favors. Your little community organizing and legal maneuvering won't stop what's coming."

Penelope felt ice flood her veins, but she kept her expression neutral. "Compulsory purchase requires demonstrating significant public benefit. You'll need more than a sympathetic judge."

"We have extensive documentation. Jobs created, infrastructure improvements, economic growth. It's quite compelling."

"Fabricated documentation isn't compelling. It's fraud."

His expression didn't change, but something cold flickered in his eyes. "Careful, Ms. Lowell. Accusations like that require proof."

"Then I'll find proof." She stood. "Now get out of my village."

"Your village?" He laughed. "You've been here two months. These people don't belong to you. They're just... temporarily distracted by your parlor tricks." He stood as well, adjusting his cufflinks. "But tricks wear off. Reality sets in. And when it does, when they realize that resisting us means missing out on life-changing money, they'll sell. Everyone does eventually."

After he left, Mrs. Bramble poured Penelope a fortifying cup of tea. "Compulsory purchase. That's serious."

"Very serious. If they actually have judicial support, it could override everything we've put in place."

"Can you stop it?"

"Maybe. If I can find evidence that their previous projects involved fraud or corruption. If I can demonstrate a pattern of misconduct." She pulled out her phone, started texting her journalist contact. "I have one week to build a case. It's not much time."

"And you're planning to leave in three days."

Penelope looked up, guilt washing over her. "The blue thread, whoever needs help..."

"Can wait a few extra days." Mrs. Bramble's voice was firm. "Penelope, I understand the impulse to help others. But Asterly is your responsibility first. Eleanor chose you to protect this place. You can't abandon that duty chasing after distant threads, no matter how desperate they seem."

"I'm not abandoning anything. I'm expanding the fight. If Omni Corp is targeting Heartstone sites globally, then helping other guardians helps us too. We're all fighting the same enemy."

"Perhaps. But if Asterly falls while you're gone, if that compulsory purchase goes through and they destroy our Heartstone, will helping some distant Seer matter?"

It was a fair question. One Penelope didn't have a good answer for.

That evening, she and Rhys sat in Eleanor's study, the blue thread visible between them and the horizon, and argued.

"Mrs. Bramble is right," Rhys said. "We should stay. Fight the compulsory purchase. Make sure Asterly is secure before we go anywhere."

"And how long will that take? Weeks? Months? Whoever's at the other end of that blue thread might not have weeks." Penelope gestured at the glowing strand. "You feel it too. The desperation. They're running out of time."

"So are we. If Omni Corp gets that compulsory purchase order..."

"Then the village fights it. With or without us. Rhys, we've given them everything they need. The land trust, the legal framework, the training. They're not helpless anymore."

"But they're not Seers. They can't do what you can do."

"No. But whoever's at the end of that blue thread is a Seer. And they're fighting alone. The way Eleanor fought alone for ten years after your grandfather died. You told me what that did to her. How it aged her, wore her down. I won't condemn another guardian to that. Not when we could help."

Rhys ran a hand through his hair, frustrated. "I'm not saying we never go. I'm saying we secure Asterly first. Make absolutely certain it can survive without us. Is that so unreasonable?"

"It's reasonable. It's also potentially fatal for whoever needs our help." She moved closer to him. "I know you're afraid. I am too. But we didn't ask for the blue thread to appear. We didn't ask to be part of a global network of guardians. But we are. And with that comes responsibility."

"Our responsibility is to Asterly."

"Our responsibility is to the Tethering Light. All of it. Not just the parts that are convenient or comfortable." She took his hand, felt the dawn-gold thread pulse between them. "Eleanor protected one Heartstone for forty-three years. She saved this place. But she never stopped the pattern. Never confronted the forces that were systematically destroying connection sites. Maybe that's our role. Not just to defend, but to fight back. To help other guardians. To build a network that can actually stand against people like Omni Corp."

Rhys was quiet for a long moment. Through their bond, Penelope could feel his conflict. His fear for Asterly, his fear for her, his reluctant acknowledgment that she might be right.

"Three days," he finally said. "We give the village three more days to prepare for our absence. We train Sarah more intensively. We make sure the land trust is bulletproof. And we brief the council on the compulsory purchase threat so they're ready to fight it. Then we go. Together."

"Together," Penelope agreed.

They spent the next seventy-two hours in a frenzy of preparation. Legal documents drafted and filed. Emergency protocols established. Sarah Mitchell trained until she could sense the Heartstone's rhythms with reasonable accuracy. The village council briefed on every possible Omni Corp tactic, armed with phone numbers for lawyers, journalists, environmental groups, anyone who could help if the situation escalated.

On the evening of the third day, they held a meeting in the Grove's parlor. Every villager who could make it came. More than thirty people crammed into the space that had once been Eleanor's sanctuary.

Penelope stood at the front of the room and explained. About the blue thread. About other Heartstones. About the global nature of the Tethering Light and the forces trying to destroy it.

"I know this sounds like I'm abandoning you," she said. "Like I'm running away just when Omni Corp is increasing pressure. But I promise you, that's not what this is. This is us joining a larger fight. Building alliances with other guardians. Learning from their experiences. And yes, helping someone who's in desperate trouble right now."

"How long will you be gone?" someone asked.

"I don't know. Two weeks? A month? It depends on what we find when we follow the blue thread."

"And if Omni Corp gets their compulsory purchase while you're away?"

"Then you fight it. You have the legal framework. You have the evidence I've gathered. You have Sarah to monitor the Heartstone. And you have each other. That's not nothing. That's powerful."

Mrs. Bramble stood. "Penelope's right. We've been depending on her to save us. But that's not fair to her, and it's not how communities survive. We need to learn to protect ourselves. To fight our own battles. She's given us the tools. Now we need to use them."

Murmurs of agreement rippled through the room.

Tom Thomas stood as well. "I say we let them go. Let them help whoever needs helping. And we hold the line here. Show Omni Corp that Asterly doesn't break just because our Seer takes a holiday."

Laughter, nervous but genuine.

One by one, villagers stood and voiced their support. Not

all of them, a few clearly worried about being left to fight alone, but most. Enough.

As the meeting dispersed, Penelope felt something shift. These weren't her dependents anymore. They were her partners. Her community. People who would fight alongside her, not just rely on her to fight for them.

That night, she and Rhys packed for the journey. Clothes, Eleanor's journals, maps, everything they might need. The blue thread pulsed urgently, as if sensing that help was finally coming.

"Are you sure about this?" Rhys asked as they worked.

"No. But I'm sure about doing nothing being worse."

"Fair point."

They finished packing in silence. Then Rhys pulled out something from his pocket. A small velvet box.

"My grandfather gave this to Eleanor when they bonded as Seer and Guardian," he said, opening it. Inside was a silver pendant. Simple, elegant, engraved with a spiral pattern. "The spiral represents the thread network. All connections leading back to the center, the Heartstone. Eleanor wore it every day for forty-three years."

He lifted the pendant and gestured for Penelope to turn around. She did, and felt his hands gentle on her neck as he fastened the clasp.

"For protection," he murmured. "And to remind you that you're not alone in this. Whatever we find at the end of that blue thread, we face it together."

Penelope touched the pendant, felt the cool silver against her skin. Through the dawn-gold thread, she felt Rhys's emotion. Complex and deep and not entirely about the Guardian bond anymore.

She turned to face him, close enough to see the silver flecks in his grey eyes, and understood that something fundamental had shifted between them. They'd started as antagonist and outsider. Become Guardian and Seer. And somewhere along the way, become something more.

She rose on her toes and kissed him.

It was tentative at first. Testing. Then deeper as Rhys's hands came up to cup her face, as the dawn-gold thread between them blazed so bright it was almost painful.

When they finally pulled apart, both breathless, Penelope whispered, "We probably shouldn't have done that."

"Probably not," Rhys agreed, his voice rough.

"Complicates things."

"Definitely."

"We should focus on the mission. On helping whoever needs help. Not on..." She gestured vaguely between them.

"Right. Focus. Mission. Not on the fact that I've wanted to do that for weeks."

"Weeks?"

"Since you mended the Patels' heartline and looked at me like you'd just discovered fire."

Despite everything, despite the danger they were about to face and the complexity they'd just added to their bond, Penelope laughed. "We're idiots."

"Complete idiots," Rhys agreed, and kissed her again.

Tomorrow they would leave Asterly. Would follow the blue thread into unknown territory. Would face dangers they couldn't yet imagine.

But tonight, in Eleanor's study with the Heartstone pulsing approval in the distant grove, they were simply two people who'd found each other against all odds. Seer and Guardian. Partners. And now, hesitantly, something more.

The blue thread pulsed urgent, but for tonight, they let it wait.

Some things, they were learning, were worth taking time for.

CHAPTER TWELVE

They left Asterly at dawn.

Penelope stood at the Grove's gate, looking back at the house that had become home in just two months. The wild garden, the sage-green door, the windows that caught morning light like prayer. It felt wrong to leave, even temporarily.

"It'll still be here when we get back," Rhys said quietly beside her.

"Will it? If Omni Corp succeeds..."

"They won't. The village is ready." He squeezed her hand. "And we're not abandoning them. We're widening the fight."

Sarah Mitchell waited by Rhys's car, looking nervous and determined in equal measure. The young woman had proven herself capable during training, but taking responsibility for the Heartstone in Penelope's absence was a heavy burden.

"You have my number," Penelope said to her. "Any problems, anything at all, call immediately."

"I will. And Ms. Lowell?" Sarah hesitated. "Thank you. For trusting me with this. My whole life, I felt like I was slightly out of step with everyone else. Like I could sense things they couldn't. Now I understand why."

"The sensitivity you have, it's a gift. Eleanor probably had it too before the Sight fully manifested. Use it well."

They drove north through the Cotswolds as the sun rose higher, following the blue thread that only Penelope could see. It stretched toward Wales, toward the coast, unwavering and urgent.

Rhys drove while Penelope studied Eleanor's journals, looking for any reference to other Heartstones or other guardians. There was surprisingly little. A few cryptic mentions of "sister sites" and "the greater network," but nothing concrete.

"My grandfather's journals might have more," Rhys said. "They're in storage at my mother's house. We could stop there, it's on the way."

"Your mother lives in Wales?"

"Near Aberystwyth. Small cottage on the coast. She's been after me to visit for months." He smiled ruefully. "This probably isn't the family reunion she was hoping for."

They stopped for lunch in a village called Hay-on-Wye, famous for its bookshops. Rhys practically vibrated with excitement as they walked the streets, ducking into shop after shop. For a few hours, they could almost pretend this was a holiday. A romantic getaway for two people who'd just admitted they cared for each other.

But the blue thread was a constant presence, pulsing urgent at the edge of Penelope's vision, reminding her why they were really here.

They reached Rhys's mother's cottage as the sun began to set. It was small and weathered, perched on a cliff overlooking the Irish Sea. Wind whipped Penelope's hair as they approached the door, carrying the salt-sharp scent of ocean.

The woman who answered was in her sixties, grey-haired and sturdy, with eyes the same storm-grey as her son's.

"Rhys!" She pulled him into a fierce hug. "About time you visited. And you must be Penelope. The London lawyer who gave up everything to protect Asterly." She held out her hand. "I'm Bronwen Penrose. Come in, come in. You both look exhausted."

Inside, the cottage was warm and cluttered. Books everywhere, of course, but also knitting projects, watercolor paintings, the comfortable chaos of someone who lived alone and liked it that way.

Bronwen made tea while Rhys explained why they'd come. His mother listened without interruption, her expression growing more serious as he described the blue thread, the other Seer in trouble, their decision to help.

"You're following in your grandfather's footsteps," she said when he finished. "He and Eleanor always said the Tethering Light needed more than isolated guardians. That we needed networks of our own to stand against the forces of severance."

"You knew?" Penelope asked. "About the Heartstones,

the threads, all of it?"

"Of course. Thomas was my father. I grew up hearing about the Tethering Light, watching him work with Eleanor. I don't have the Sight myself, never did. But I believe in what they were doing. What you're doing now." She stood. "Come. I'll show you Thomas's journals. He documented everything. Including information about other Heartstone sites he'd heard of."

She led them to a small study where shelves held dozens of leather-bound journals. Bronwen pulled down three volumes from a specific year. "These are from 1994 through 1996. Thomas was doing research on the global network. He'd made contact with several other guardians, exchanged letters, even visited a few sites."

Penelope opened the first journal and found exactly what she'd hoped for. Maps. Names. Locations of other Heartstones across the UK and Europe. And notes about the guardians protecting them.

"This is incredible," she murmured, flipping pages. "He documented seventeen different sites."

"Seventeen that he knew of," Bronwen corrected. "He suspected there were more. Hundreds, perhaps, scattered across the world. But these were the ones he had confirmed contact with."

Rhys leaned over Penelope's shoulder, reading. "Most of these sites are still marked as active. But three have notation. 'Connection lost, 1989.' 'Severed, 1992.' 'Guardian deceased, no successor, 1995.' Did he investigate what happened to them?"

"He tried. But by then, he was already ill. The same cancer that eventually killed him. Eleanor wanted him to focus on recovering, not chasing after distant Heartstones." Bronwen's expression was sad. "He died believing he'd failed them. Failed to build the network that could have protected those sites."

"He didn't fail," Penelope said firmly. "He laid the groundwork. And now we're finishing what he started."

They spent the evening poring over Thomas's journals, compiling information. The blue thread led toward North Wales, toward a coastal town called Penmaenmawr. And in Thomas's notes, there was a reference to that exact location.

Penmaenmawr Heartstone, Guardian: Rhian Davies. Strong Seer, fiercely independent. Refused assistance when offered. Site shows signs of degradation but Davies insists she can manage alone.

The note was dated 2001. Twenty-four years ago.

"If Rhian Davies is still the guardian, she'd be in her seventies by now," Penelope said. "Maybe older. Managing a Heartstone alone at that age..."

"Would be nearly impossible," Rhys finished. "Especially if Omni Corp or whoever is targeting the site."

They left early the next morning, armed with Thomas's journals and Bronwen's blessing. The older woman hugged them both fiercely at the door.

"Be careful," she said. "And Rhys? Don't wait another two months to visit. Even if you're not chasing mystical distress signals."

"I promise, Mum."

The drive to Penmaenmawr took three hours through increasingly dramatic landscape. Mountains rose on either side of the road, and the Irish Sea glittered cold and grey to their left. The blue thread grew stronger as they approached, pulsing with desperate urgency.

They found the town nestled between mountains and sea. Small, picturesque, the kind of place tourists loved but locals found claustrophobic. The blue thread led them to a cottage on the outskirts, perched precariously on a hillside overlooking the water.

Penelope knocked on the weathered door. No answer.

She knocked again, harder.

Finally, movement inside. The door opened a crack, revealing a woman who must have been Rhian Davies. She was elderly, probably in her eighties, with white hair and eyes that had once been sharp but were now clouded with exhaustion.

"I don't want whatever you're selling," she said, starting to close the door.

"We're not selling anything," Penelope said quickly. "We're guardians. From Asterly. We saw your thread. The blue one. You called for help."

Rhian froze. Then, slowly, opened the door wider. "You're real. I'd stopped believing anyone would come."

"We're real. And we're here to help."

Rhian Davies looked at them for a long moment, something like hope flickering in her tired eyes. Then she stepped aside.

"You'd better come in. We don't have much time."

CHAPTER THIRTEEN

Rhian Davies's cottage smelled of lavender and desperation. The elderly woman led them through a narrow hallway cluttered with books and papers, past a kitchen where unwashed dishes filled the sink, into a parlor that might once have been cozy. Now it felt like a fortress under siege.

"I stopped answering the door three weeks ago," Rhian said, her voice thin with exhaustion. "Too many visitors. Too many offers. Too much pressure." She sank into an armchair, her white hair escaping its bun, her hands trembling. "I knew they'd come eventually. I just didn't think it would be this aggressive."

Penelope sat on the worn sofa, Rhys beside her. Through the dusty window, she could see Penmaenmawr stretching down the hillside toward the sea. Even from here, she could sense it. Wrong threads. Damaged connections. The network here was sick.

"Tell us what happened," Penelope said gently.

Rhian closed her eyes. "It started six months ago. A development company, 'Coastal Futures Ltd.' They came with beautiful plans. A luxury resort on the headland. Premium homes. Marina expansion. They said it would bring jobs, prosperity, save the dying town." Her laugh was bitter. "But I could See what they were really doing. Severing threads. Breaking bonds. Turning a community into a commodity."

"Did you try to stop them?"

"Of course I tried. I'm the guardian here. This is my responsibility." Rhian's hands clenched in her lap. "But I'm eighty-three years old. I haven't had a Guardian partner since my husband died fifteen years ago. I can See the threads, but I don't have the strength to mend them all. Not anymore."

Penelope felt the weight of that admission. Eleanor had lasted ten years alone. Rhian had endured fifteen.

"How many families have sold?" Rhys asked.

"Eleven. Out of a community of forty-eight households." Rhian opened her eyes, and they were haunted. "Each sale weakens the network. Each family that leaves takes their threads with them. The Heartstone is dying, and I can't stop it."

"Where is your Heartstone?" Penelope stood. "Can I see it?"

"In the back garden. Follow me."

They walked through the cluttered house to a small garden that backed onto the hillside. And there, half-hidden by overgrown heather and gorse, sat a stone circle. Ancient.

Weathered. At its center, a Heartstone the size of a small boulder, its light barely visible in the afternoon sun.

Penelope opened the Sight fully.

The Heartstone was grey. Dying. Threads extended from it toward the village below, but they were thin, frayed, many of them severed completely. It looked like a spider's web after a storm, beautiful structure torn apart, barely holding together.

"Oh," she breathed. "Rhian, this is..."

"Terminal. I know." The old woman's voice cracked. "I've held it together as long as I could. But it's too much. Too many breaks. Too much damage. I sent out that blue thread three months ago, hoping someone would see it. Hoping another Seer existed somewhere. I'd almost given up believing the old stories about a network of guardians."

Penelope knelt beside the Heartstone, placing her palm against its cool surface. She could feel it struggling. Feel it trying to maintain connections that were being actively severed.

"They're still pressuring people," she realized. "The development company. They're targeting specific families. The ones whose threads are strongest."

"Yes. They're methodical. Strategic." Rhian joined her, her own weathered hand touching the stone. "If they get three more households, the network collapses entirely. And once the Heartstone goes dark, there's nothing holding the community together. Within a generation, this place becomes just another forgotten seaside town."

Rhys crouched beside them. "Who's behind it? The development company."

"I don't know. They use local representatives, smiling people with contracts and promises. But I can sense something bigger behind them. Something that understands what they're doing. This isn't random development. This is targeted severance."

Penelope's mind raced through the possibilities. "Omni Corporation has a subsidiary called 'Community Futures Ltd.' I wouldn't be surprised if 'Coastal Futures' is related."

"You've dealt with them before?"

"We're dealing with them now. In Asterly. They tried to buy up our village too." Penelope stood, determination crystallizing. "But we stopped them. Formed a community land trust. Made the village legally difficult to break up. And we can help you do the same here."

Rhian looked up at her with something like hope flickering in tired eyes. "You can mend this? You have that kind of power?"

"Not alone. But with Rhys anchoring me, yes. I can strengthen the damaged threads. And we can teach your community how to protect themselves legally and emotionally." Penelope helped the elderly woman to her feet. "But first, I need to stabilize your Heartstone. It's too weak. If we're going to fight, we need a strong foundation."

"I don't understand. How do you stabilize a Heartstone?"

"Watch."

Penelope placed both hands on the Heartstone and opened herself fully to the Sight. The network blazed into visibility around her: every thread, every connection, every break. It was overwhelming. Asterly's network was healthy, easy to navigate. This was chaos.

She felt Rhys's hand on her shoulder. Instantly, the dawn-gold bond between them flared bright, steadying her. Anchoring her.

"I've got you," he murmured. "Find the core."

She dove deeper, past the damaged outer threads, past the severed connections, searching for the heart of the network. And there, buried beneath layers of decay, she found it. A cluster of bronze and silver threads. Family bonds. Old friendships. Connections that had survived despite everything.

These were strong. Unbreakable. The people who would never sell, never leave, no matter what was offered.

"There are still strong threads," she said aloud. "Not many, but they're brilliant. Determined."

"Use them," Rhys said. "Let them feed power back into the stone."

Penelope focused on those bright threads, those loyal connections. She gathered them, mentally braiding them together, and channeled their strength back into the Heartstone itself.

The grey stone began to glow.

Faintly at first, then brighter. Pearl luminescence spreading from its core outward. The dying threads that still connected to it began to strengthen, drawing on the renewed power.

It wasn't enough to heal everything. But it was enough to stop the bleeding.

Penelope released the connection and staggered. Rhys caught her before she fell.

"How do you feel?" he asked.

"Like I just ran a marathon." She leaned against him, breathing hard. "But look."

The Heartstone glowed steady now. Not brilliant, not healthy, but alive. Fighting. The village network visible around it, damaged but no longer dying.

Rhian Davies stood staring at her Heartstone, tears streaming down her weathered face. "You did in five minutes what I couldn't do in six months."

"I had help." Penelope straightened, though her legs still trembled. "And I had training Eleanor and Rhys gave me. But Rhian, this is only temporary. The Heartstone will start to fade again unless we address the root cause."

"The development company."

"Yes. We need to stop them from acquiring more property. And we need to strengthen the community's resolve to stay connected." Penelope moved toward the cottage. "Do you have a list? Of the families still here? The ones who haven't sold?"

"In my study. Why?"

"Because we're going to visit every single one. We're going to show them what they have. What they're protecting. And we're going to teach them how to fight."

They worked through the evening and into the night. Rhian provided names, addresses, family histories. Penelope and Rhys studied maps of the village, identified the key thread nexus points, the families whose connections were strongest.

"The Williams family," Rhian pointed to a house on the map. "Four generations in that cottage. Their family bonds are like steel cables. If they sell, five other families will follow."

"Then we start with them," Penelope decided. "Tomorrow morning. We show them exactly what they have. What they'll lose."

"You're going to reveal the threads? The Tethering Light?" Rhian looked shocked. "Eleanor always said we should keep it secret. That people weren't ready."

"Eleanor was alone and afraid of being thought mad. We're not alone. And times have changed." Penelope met the old woman's eyes. "People are starving for connection. For proof that their relationships matter. We're going to give them that proof. Show them the network they're part of. Make them understand what they're protecting."

Rhys nodded slowly. "It's risky. But it worked in Asterly. When people saw the threads, understood what they were, they fought harder to preserve them."

"It could also backfire," Rhian warned. "Some people, when they See, they panic. They deny. They convince themselves it's mass hysteria."

"Then we'll deal with that if it happens. But doing nothing means watching your Heartstone die." Penelope stood, exhaustion pulling at her. "We start tomorrow. Nine AM. The Williams family first."

Rhian showed them to a small guest room with a double bed. Penelope was too tired to be embarrassed about the sleeping arrangements. She and Rhys collapsed onto the mattress still fully clothed, the dawn-gold thread between them pulsing warm and certain.

"You were brilliant today," Rhys murmured, his arm around her shoulders.

"I'm terrified this won't work."

"It'll work. Look what you did in Asterly. This is just... a bigger version of that."

"Much bigger. And if we fail, Rhian loses everything."

"We won't fail." He kissed her forehead. "Sleep. Tomorrow we save a village."

Penelope closed her eyes, listening to the distant sound of waves against the Welsh coast. Somewhere below, the Heartstone glowed in its ancient circle, holding on, fighting.

Tomorrow they would help it fight back.

CHAPTER FOURTEEN

The Williams family cottage sat at the high point of Penmaenmawr, overlooking both the sea and the village. Four generations lived there: grandmother Margaret, her son David and his wife Helen, their daughter Sophie and her two young children. The family threads connecting them were visible from the road, a complex web of crimson and bronze.

Penelope knocked on the door at nine AM sharp, Rhys and Rhian flanking her.

Margaret Williams answered, suspicious eyes assessing them. "Whatever you're selling, we're not interested."

"We're not selling anything," Penelope said quickly. "I'm Penelope Lowell, from Asterly in the Cotswolds. This is Rhys Penrose, and you know Rhian. We're here to show you something. Something that might change your mind about the development offers you've been receiving."

"We haven't accepted any offers."

"I know. And we're here to make sure you don't have to."

Penelope met the older woman's gaze steadily. "Five minutes. That's all we ask. If you're not interested after that, we'll leave and never bother you again."

Margaret studied them for a long moment, then stepped aside. "Five minutes. But I'm timing you."

The family gathered in the living room, curious and wary. David and Helen sat on the sofa, Sophie in an armchair with her youngest daughter on her lap. The older child, a boy of about eight, sat cross-legged on the floor.

Penelope took a breath. This was the moment. Either they'd believe, or they'd think she was mad.

"What I'm about to show you will seem impossible," she began. "You'll want to deny it, rationalize it away, convince yourself you're hallucinating. But I promise you, it's real. And once you've seen it, you'll understand why your community is worth fighting for."

"Just get on with it," Margaret said gruffly. "Clock's ticking."

Penelope opened herself to the Sight. Then, through the dawn-gold bond, she channeled it to Rhys. He gasped slightly, then steadied, becoming her anchor. Together, they reached out to the Williams family.

And showed them the threads.

Sophie screamed. David swore. Helen clutched her husband's arm, her eyes wide with shock. Even Margaret stumbled backward, her hand finding the wall for support.

Only the eight-year-old boy seemed delighted. "Mummy!

Look! We're all glowing!"

Because they were. The family blazed with connections. Crimson threads between parents and children. Bronze bonds between siblings. Silver strands linking them to their home, their land, their history. And stretching out from their cottage, gossamer threads connecting them to neighbors, friends, the village itself.

"What is this?" Margaret's voice shook. "What are you doing to us?"

"Nothing. I'm just making visible what was always there." Penelope kept her voice calm, steady. "These are threads of connection. Bonds of love, loyalty, friendship, belonging. Everyone has them. Most people never see them. But they're real. And they're what makes you a family. What makes Penmaenmawr a community instead of just a collection of houses."

David stood, reaching out tentatively toward the crimson thread connecting him to his mother. His fingers passed through it, but he could feel it. Warmth. Certainty. Love.

"This is insane," he whispered. "This can't be real."

"It is real," Rhian said, stepping forward. "I've seen these threads my entire life. Your grandmother saw them too, Margaret. She was a sensitive. She never spoke of it, but she knew. She felt the connections."

Margaret's eyes widened. "My mother... she used to say she could 'feel' when something was wrong in the village. When people were fighting or hurting. I thought she was just intuitive."

"She was. But she was also seeing this network, in her own way." Penelope gestured to the window. "And right now, that network is under attack. Every family that sells to the development company severs their threads. Weakens the whole web. If enough people leave, the entire network collapses. And then you're not a community anymore. You're just strangers living near each other."

Sophie was crying, staring at the threads connecting her to her children. "How long will we be able to see this?"

"Only as long as I'm maintaining it. But once you've seen, you'll remember. You'll feel the connections even when you can't see them." Penelope released the Sight gradually, letting the threads fade. "And you'll understand what you're protecting when you refuse to sell."

The family sat in stunned silence.

Then the eight-year-old boy spoke up. "I don't want the glowing to go away. Can we keep it?"

His innocence broke the tension. Helen laughed, pulling him close. "No, sweetheart. But now we know it's there."

David turned to Penelope. "Coastal Futures has been pressuring us for three months. They've offered twice what our cottage is worth. My wife and I have been tempted. The money would change our lives."

"It would. But at what cost?" Penelope moved to the window, looking out over the village. "Money is easy to earn back. Community, real connection, true belonging, those are irreplaceable. Once severed, those threads take generations to rebuild. If they ever do."

Margaret spoke, her voice firm despite her trembling hands. "We're not selling. We weren't planning to anyway, but now... after seeing that..." She shook her head. "This is our home. Our family's home. No amount of money is worth giving that up."

"Good." Rhys pulled out a folder. "Then we need your help. We have legal documents, a model for a community land trust. If we can get twenty families to join, we can make Penmaenmawr legally resistant to buyouts. Make it difficult for developers to break you apart."

They spent the next hour explaining the trust, answering questions, showing them the Asterly model. By the time they left, Margaret had agreed to host a community meeting. To invite the other families who hadn't sold yet.

"One down," Rhys said as they walked back down the hill. "How many more?"

"Rhian identified thirty-seven households still here," Penelope said. "We need at least twenty for the trust to work. So we need to convince nineteen more."

"We have four days," Rhian said quietly. "Coastal Futures is having a final 'information session' on Friday. They're bringing architects, showing final plans, making their last big push. If they get commitments from three more families, the network fails."

"Then we work fast." Penelope pulled out the list. "Next is the Chen family. Then the Patels. Then the Harrisons."

"Wait," Rhys said. "Patels and Harrisons? Like in Asterly?"

"Different families, same surnames." Rhian smiled slightly. "It's Wales. Half the village has ten surnames between them."

They worked through the morning and into the afternoon, visiting family after family. Each time, Penelope revealed the threads. Each time, people gasped, denied, then finally accepted what they were seeing.

Some were moved to tears. Others were angry that they'd never been told. A few were frightened. But none of them, once they'd Seen the network, wanted to sever their part of it.

By evening, they had commitments from eighteen families. Two short of what they needed.

"The Jenkins and the O'Malleys are our last hope," Rhian said as they gathered in her parlor. "Both families have been seriously considering selling. The Jenkins have medical bills. The O'Malleys want to move closer to their son in Cardiff. I don't know if seeing the threads will be enough."

"Then we offer more than just sight," Penelope said. "We offer solutions. The community trust can help with medical bills. And the O'Malleys... maybe they don't have to move. Maybe their son can visit more. Maybe there's another way."

They visited the Jenkins family that evening. Showed them the threads. Explained how the community trust could create a support fund for medical emergencies. By the end, Mr. Jenkins was weeping, his wife holding him, and they'd agreed to stay.

Nineteen families. One to go.

The O'Malley house was dark when they arrived. No one answered the door.

"They've already left," a neighbor called from across the street. "Signed the papers this morning. Moving to Cardiff next week."

Penelope felt the thread break. Actually felt it. A silver connection between the O'Malley house and the village network snapped, withering, disappearing. The Heartstone on the hillside pulsed once with pain.

"We're one short," Rhys said quietly.

"Then we find another family." Penelope turned to Rhian. "You said eleven sold. But there are sixty households total in this village. That means we're missing more than just the O'Malleys. Who else is here that we haven't visited?"

Rhian thought for a moment. "The artists' collective. Twenty-something creatives who bought the old hotel on the headland five years ago. They keep to themselves mostly. I didn't think to include them because they're not native to Penmaenmawr."

"But they live here. They're part of the community, even if they don't realize it yet." Penelope started walking toward the headland. "Take us there."

The old hotel had been converted into a stunning live-work space. Art studios on the ground floor, living quarters above. Music drifted from open windows, along with the smell of paint and creativity.

A woman in her thirties answered their knock, paint-splattered overalls, curious expression. "Can I help you?"

"I hope so," Penelope said. "My name is Penelope Lowell. We're trying to save this village. And we need your help."

They gathered the collective in the main common room. Twenty-three young artists, musicians, writers, all looking skeptical but interested.

Penelope didn't bother with explanations. She just showed them.

The threads blazed into visibility. The artists gasped, then began talking all at once. For them, this wasn't frightening. It was beautiful. Inspiring. Proof that the creative community they'd built was real, tangible, worth preserving.

"This is incredible," breathed a young man with a sketchpad, already trying to draw what he was seeing. "How is this possible?"

"It's always been there. I'm just making it visible." Penelope released the Sight slowly. "And it's under threat. The development company wants this headland for their resort. If they get it, your collective dissolves. The connections you've built here, the creative community that makes your work possible, all of it disappears."

"We got an offer," the woman in overalls said. "Last week. It was... substantial."

"I'm sure it was. But can you recreate this elsewhere?" Penelope gestured around the room. "This specific combination of people, this exact alchemy of creativity, this particular magic you've built together?"

The artists looked at each other. Silent conversations happening through glances and nods.

"No," the woman said finally. "We can't. This is... this is unique. Special."

"Then join our community land trust. Help us protect Penmaenmawr. Not just the historical families, but the new ones too. The creative community you've built here, it's part of the network now. Part of what makes this place alive."

The artists voted. It took ten minutes. The decision was unanimous.

They would stay. They would join the trust.

Twenty families. Enough to make it work.

The community meeting on Friday evening drew fifty people. Margaret Williams stood at the front of the village hall, next to Penelope and Rhys.

"I called you all here because I've seen something," Margaret began. "Something that changed how I think about this village, about our community, about what we stand to lose if we let developers tear us apart."

She told her story. Others stood to tell theirs. The Chen family. The Patels. The artists' collective. One by one, people who had Seen the threads shared their experiences.

And then Penelope stood.

"Coastal Futures will tell you they're offering you a better life. Money. Opportunity. Escape. But what they're really offering is disconnection. Severance. The breaking of bonds that took generations to build." She looked around the room. "I'm from Asterly. We faced the same threat. And we fought back. We formed a community land trust, exactly like the one we're proposing here. It worked. We're still together. Still connected. Still a community."

"But what about those of us who need the money?" someone called from the back. "Medical bills, failing businesses, children to support?"

"The trust can help. It's not just about preventing sales. It's about supporting each other. Creating a support network that helps families stay here without financial ruin." Rhys stepped forward with documents. "We've drafted bylaws. Created a support fund. Established legal protections. This isn't just defense. It's community building."

The vote took an hour. There were arguments, concerns, fears.

But in the end, forty-two families voted to join the trust. Coastal Futures would face a legally unified community, not isolated property owners.

The network would survive.

That night, Penelope and Rhys stood at Rhian's Heartstone. It glowed steady and strong, pearl luminescence spreading across the hillside. The threads connecting it to the village blazed bright, woven together, reinforced by shared purpose and renewed community.

"You did it," Rhian said, tears streaming down her face. "You saved us."

"You sent out that blue thread," Penelope reminded her. "You called for help. We just answered."

The elderly woman took Penelope's hands. "There are others. Other Heartstones. Other guardians struggling alone. If you could do this for me, you could do it for them."

"That's what we're planning." Rhys showed her Thomas's journals, the list of sites his grandfather had documented. "We're going to build a network. Connect guardians who've been isolated. Help them protect their communities."

Rhian nodded slowly. "Like Eleanor and Thomas wanted. A true network of guardians." She squeezed Penelope's hands. "I'll help. However I can. Even if I'm too old to travel, I can coordinate, communicate, train younger seers."

"We'll need that," Penelope said. "Because this is bigger than any one village. Bigger than any one Heartstone. The forces of severance are organized. Global. We need to match that scale."

They stood together in the stone circle, three guardians under the Welsh stars, planning a revolution.

Somewhere, in cities and towns across the world, other Heartstones pulsed. Other seers struggled alone. Other communities faced the same threats.

But now, finally, they wouldn't have to fight alone.

The Guardian Network was being born.

CHAPTER FIFTEEN

They stayed in Penmaenmawr for three more days.

Penelope worked with the newly formed community land trust, showing them how to file paperwork, set up support structures, create communication networks. Rhys helped Sarah Mitchell remotely coordinate Asterly's protection, ensuring their own village remained secure in their absence.

And Rhian, energized by the victory, became a teacher herself. She showed Penelope advanced techniques Eleanor had never documented. How to sense breaks in the network before they became critical. How to strengthen threads without exhausting herself. How to read the pulses of a Heartstone to predict community health.

"Eleanor was brilliant," Rhian said on their last evening, sitting in her garden by the now-glowing Heartstone. "But she was isolated. Afraid. She never connected with other guardians, never learned their techniques. If she had, she might still be alive."

"Why didn't she?" Penelope asked. "If Thomas knew

about other Heartstones, other seers, why didn't they build a network?"

"Fear, mostly. Fear that revealing ourselves would bring attention. Fear that the forces of severance would target us if we organized." Rhian's weathered face was sad. "Eleanor and Thomas tried to contact other guardians in the late 1990s. Sent letters, made calls. Out of seventeen sites Thomas had documented, only three responded. And of those three, two refused to help. Said it was too dangerous to connect."

"What happened to the third?"

"The guardian died in a car accident six months after agreeing to work with them. Eleanor became convinced their attempt to organize had drawn attention. Made them targets. She stopped reaching out after that."

Penelope absorbed this, watching the threads pulse around the Heartstone. "That's why she never found me until it was too late. She was afraid to look for help."

"And I repeated her mistake," Rhian admitted. "I've been alone for fifteen years, too frightened to send out that blue thread. Too afraid that calling for help would make things worse." She looked at Penelope with fierce intensity. "Promise me you won't make the same error. Promise me you'll build the network Eleanor was too frightened to create."

"I promise."

On the morning of their departure, the Williams family brought scones. The Chen family brought tea. The artists' collective brought a painting, a visual representation of the thread network they'd seen, abstract and beautiful.

"Come back and visit," Margaret Williams said, embracing Penelope. "Don't be strangers. You're part of this community now, whether you live here or not."

Penelope felt the truth of it. A thread connected her to Penmaenmawr now. Faint, silver, but real. She'd helped save this place. It was part of her network too.

As they drove away, Rhian standing at her gate waving, Penelope turned to Rhys. "We can't do this one village at a time. It's too slow. If Omni Corp or whoever is behind them is targeting multiple sites simultaneously, we need a faster response."

"What are you thinking?"

"A real network. Not just us traveling to each threatened site, but guardians teaching guardians. Sites helping each other. Communication systems. Early warning signals." She pulled out Thomas's journals. "He documented seventeen sites. Some may be lost, but if even half are still active, that's eight or nine potential guardians we can connect with."

"And if they're like Eleanor and Rhian? Too afraid to work together?"

"Then we show them it works. We show them Asterly and Penmaenmawr standing strong because we helped them organize." Penelope's mind was racing now, seeing the possibilities. "We could create a communication network. Regular check-ins. Shared resources. Legal templates for community land trusts. Training programs for new seers."

Rhys smiled. "You're talking about building an organization."

"I'm talking about building what Eleanor and Thomas wanted but were too afraid to create. A Guardian Network that actually works together. That protects each other."

They drove south through Wales, the landscape shifting from coastal beauty to rolling hills. Penelope made notes, filling pages with ideas, structures, systems. By the time they reached the border into England, she had the skeleton of a plan.

"We start with Thomas's list," she said. "We visit each site. Not to take over, but to offer connection. To show them they're not alone."

"That could take months."

"Then it takes months. But we do it right. We build trust. We prove the network works." She looked at him, the dawn-gold thread between them pulsing bright and certain. "Unless you think it's too much? Too ambitious?"

"I think it's exactly what we should be doing." He took her hand. "Eleanor protected one Heartstone for forty-three years. Rhian protected one for sixty-five. Imagine what we could do if we protected dozens. Hundreds."

"Transform communities. Make severance harder. Show people that connection matters." Penelope felt the weight and rightness of it. "This is bigger than Asterly. Bigger than any one village."

"This is the work of a lifetime."

"Good. Because I'm planning on a long one."

They returned to Asterly three days before Christmas. The village welcomed them like heroes. Sarah Mitchell reported only minor thread disturbances while they'd been gone, nothing she couldn't handle. The community land trust was functioning perfectly. Omni Corp hadn't made any new moves.

But something had changed in Penelope. She looked at Asterly differently now. Not as the only place that needed protection, but as the first place. The model. The proof of concept.

On Christmas Eve, she and Rhys stood in the oak grove at Sunlit Grove, the Heartstone glowing warmly in the winter darkness.

"I've been thinking," Rhys said quietly. "If we're going to travel to other sites, we need someone here. A permanent guardian for Asterly."

"Sarah's good, but she's not a seer."

"No. But she has sensitivity. And she has four siblings, all with varying degrees of talent. One of them, her younger sister Emma, she has the Sight. I'm sure of it. She just doesn't know it yet."

"Can we train her?"

"You can. She trusts you. The village trusts you." He turned to face her fully. "Train her this winter. Find her a Guardian partner. Establish her as Asterly's protector. And then, in spring, we go. We visit the other sites. We build the network."

Penelope felt the rightness of it. "That gives us three months. Is it enough time?"

"To train a new seer? Barely. But Eleanor trained you in

days. You can train Emma in months."

"And what about Asterly while we're gone? What if something happens?"

"Then we come back. Or we send help from one of the other sites we've connected with. That's the point of a network, Penelope. No one has to be alone anymore."

She kissed him, the winter stars brilliant above them, the Heartstone pulsing approval. "Spring, then. We build the network in spring."

January passed in a blur of training. Emma Mitchell was twenty-one, university graduate, back home and uncertain what to do with her life. When Penelope showed her the threads for the first time, the young woman didn't scream or deny. She laughed with pure joy.

"I knew it," Emma breathed, watching the golden network blaze around her. "I've always felt it. My whole life, I've sensed connections between people, between places. I thought I was just overly empathetic. But this... this is real."

"It's real. And it's your inheritance now. If you want it."

Emma didn't hesitate. "Teach me everything."

Penelope taught her control, focus, how to strengthen threads and sense breaks. Found her a Guardian partner, a young man named Oliver Chen who'd grown up in the village, who had the same quiet strength Rhys possessed.

By February, Emma could maintain the Heartstone alone for hours. By early March, she was performing thread repairs without supervision.

"She's ready," Penelope told the village council on the first day of spring. "Emma Mitchell is Asterly's new primary guardian. Sarah will support her. Oliver will anchor her. And Rhys and I... we're expanding the work."

Mrs. Bramble, now chair of the community land trust, nodded approvingly. "You're going to help other villages."

"Yes. Build a network of guardians. So no one has to fight alone like Eleanor did. Like Rhian did."

"How long will you be gone?"

"We don't know. Months, probably. Maybe longer. But we'll come back regularly. Check in. Help if needed." Penelope looked around at the faces she'd come to love. "Asterly is home. It always will be. But there are other homes out there that need help too."

Maeve wiped her eyes. "Eleanor would be so proud of you."

"I hope so."

They left on a brilliant spring morning, the wild garden at Sunlit Grove in full bloom. Emma and Oliver stood at the gate, ready to take over protection. The village gathered in the square to see them off.

"First stop?" Rhys asked as they drove away.

Penelope consulted Thomas's journals. "Scotland. A site near Inverness. Guardian name: Moira MacLeod. Last contact: 2005."

"Twenty years ago. She might not even be there anymore."

"Then we find out who took over. Or we help establish a new guardian." Penelope watched Asterly disappear in the rearview mirror. "Either way, we're building the network. One Heartstone at a time."

The road stretched ahead of them, spring sunlight warming the English countryside. Somewhere in Scotland, a guardian struggled alone, not knowing help was coming. Somewhere across Britain, across Europe, across the world, Heartstones pulsed and faded, their protectors fighting alone.

But not for much longer.

The Guardian Network was coming.

And Penelope Lowell, once a corporate lawyer who believed only in facts and evidence, was leading it.

She thought Eleanor would approve.

CHAPTER SIXTEEN

Spring arrived in Asterly with sudden, violent beauty.

Four months since Christmas, and the Guardian Network had grown from nine sites to seventeen. New guardians emerging, old sites being rediscovered, the web of connections spreading across the UK and into Ireland. Penelope spent half her time traveling, meeting guardians, helping establish communication protocols, teaching the techniques she and Rhys had developed.

But Omni Corp hadn't been idle either.

In March, they'd successfully developed two more sites. Communities in Yorkshire and Cornwall, both with Heartstones, both now converted into luxury developments with generic architecture and severed threads. The guardians hadn't been killed, just made irrelevant. The Heartstones left in place but isolated, their power waning without community connection to sustain them.

It was a new tactic. More insidious than destruction. Let the sites exist but render them meaningless. Ghost Heartstones maintaining ghost communities.

Penelope stood in Eleanor's study on a mild April morning, staring at the map on the wall where she'd marked every known site. Green pins for active and healthy. Yellow for active but struggling. Red for sites under immediate threat. And black for sites already lost.

Too many black pins.

"We're losing," she said to Rhys, who was reading correspondence from Moira MacLeod.

"We're not losing. We're just not winning as fast as they're attacking."

"That's the same thing."

He set down the letter and moved to stand beside her, looking at the map. "What do you need?"

"More guardians. More sites. More resources. An actual strategy beyond reactive defense."

"So let's build one."

Over the next week, they convened the first formal gathering of the Guardian Network. Fifteen guardians traveled to Asterly, ranging from Moira MacLeod at ninety-three to a teenager named Tom Brennan from Dublin who'd just manifested the Sight six months ago.

They met in Sunlit Grove's dining room, the long table that Eleanor had probably never used for its intended purpose now hosting a council of war.

Penelope stood at the head of the table. "We've been fighting defensively. Responding to threats as they emerge. But Omni Corp is strategic. They identify weak sites, isolate them, overwhelm them before help can arrive. We need to change our approach."

"How?" David Chen asked. "We're scattered across hundreds of miles. They have resources we don't have."

"We have something they don't have. We have the threads. We have community. We have the ability to show people what matters." She gestured to Rhys, who pulled up a presentation on his laptop.

"This is Omni Corp's development pattern over the last decade," he explained, showing a timeline. "They target three to four sites per year. Always rural. Always places with strong community identity. And always following the same playbook: anonymous property purchases, legal pressure, compulsory purchase orders if necessary."

"We've been trying to defend every site," Penelope continued. "But we can't. There aren't enough of us, and we're stretched too thin. So instead, we focus our defense on the most strategically important sites. Places where winning would hurt Omni Corp's momentum. Force them to reconsider the campaign."

"Which sites?" Rhian Davies asked.

Penelope pointed to the map. Three sites circled in purple. "Glastonbury, Stonehaven, and Whitby. All three have strong Heartstones, large populations, significant cultural importance. If Omni Corp can develop these, they prove that no site is too important to touch. But if we can defend all three successfully, we prove they can be stopped."

"That's ambitious," Moira said. "Three simultaneous defenses?"

"Which is why we need to divide resources. Teams of guardians working together, supporting local efforts, using every tool we have. Legal challenges, community organizing, strategic use of the Sight."

The guardians debated for hours. Some loved the plan. Others worried it left smaller sites vulnerable. But eventually, consensus emerged. They would make their stand at Glastonbury, Stonehaven, and Whitby. Show Omni Corp that the days of picking off isolated targets were over.

As the meeting broke up, Moira pulled Penelope aside. "There's something else you need to know. I've been corresponding with guardians in Europe. France, Germany, Spain. Omni Corp isn't just a UK phenomenon. They're operating globally. Different names, different subsidiaries, but the same pattern."

"How many sites?"

"Dozens. Maybe hundreds. And they're all fighting alone, the way we were before you started organizing."

The scale of it was staggering. Penelope had been thinking nationally. But if the threat was global, if Heartstones worldwide were under attack, then the Guardian Network needed to expand far beyond the UK.

"We need to reach out," she said. "Connect with European guardians. Build a continental network."

"That's a lot of work."

"So was organizing the UK, and we did it. We just need time."

But time was something they didn't have.

Two weeks after the gathering, Omni Corp made their move. Simultaneous legal actions at all three target sites. Compulsory purchase orders filed. Development proposals submitted. Politicians lobbied. It was coordinated, aggressive, and clearly designed to overwhelm the defenders.

Penelope split the guardian resources. She and Rhys took Glastonbury, the most legally complex case. Rhian and David took Stonehaven, where community organizing would be critical. Moira and Tom Brennan took Whitby, where the Heartstone's power was strongest and could be leveraged most effectively.

The battle for Glastonbury was brutal.

Penelope spent six weeks in legal combat. Filings and counter-filings. Emergency injunctions. Environmental reviews. She used every trick she'd learned in corporate law, every contact she'd maintained, every favor she could call in. And she used the Sight strategically, showing key decision-makers the threads they were about to sever.

Rhys worked the community angle. Organizing protests, gathering petition signatures, arranging meetings where residents could see the threads for themselves. Helping them understand what development would cost.

But Omni Corp had learned from past defeats. They'd brought in better lawyers, more sympathetic judges, politicians who owed them favors. They weren't going to lose through legal maneuvering alone.

On a warm May evening, six weeks into the fight, Penelope sat in a Glastonbury hotel room with Rhys, both of them exhausted.

"We're going to lose," she said. "I can feel it. The compulsory purchase order is going to be approved. We've delayed it, made them work for it, but they're going to win."

"Then we use the nuclear option."

She looked at him. "What nuclear option?"

"We show everyone. Not just decision-makers. Not just community leaders. Everyone in Glastonbury. Every resident, every tourist, everyone within range of the Heartstone. We do what we did in Penmaenmawr, but bigger. Make the threads visible to the entire town for long enough that no one can deny what's at stake."

"That could damage the Heartstone permanently. Maybe destroy it entirely."

"And if we don't, Omni Corp will definitely destroy it. At least this way, we go down fighting."

Penelope thought about it. About the risk. About Eleanor's forty-three years of careful, measured guardianship. About the difference between preservation and sacrifice.

"We'll need the other guardians' approval. This affects everyone."

They made the calls. To Rhian, to David, to Moira. Explaining the plan, the risks, the potential consequences.

The vote was unanimous. Do it.

On the Summer Solstice, when Glastonbury was packed with tourists and residents alike, when the Heartstone's power was at its peak, they executed the working.

It took all fifteen guardians linked together. A chain of Seers and sensitives, channeling power through Penelope as the focal point. Rhys anchoring her, the dawn-gold thread blazing so bright it hurt to see.

For ten minutes, everyone in Glastonbury could see the threads.

Gold and silver and bronze and crimson, weaving through the ancient town. Connecting people to place, past to present, individual to community. The full majesty of the Tethering Light, visible to every eye.

Tourists wept. Residents stood transfixed. And the developers, the politicians, the decision-makers who'd been arguing for progress and profit, fell silent as they understood what they'd been about to destroy.

The compulsory purchase order was withdrawn the next day.

Stonehaven and Whitby followed similar patterns. Different tactics, different challenges, but the same result. Communities waking up to what they had. Fighting back. Refusing to let connection be severed for profit.

By the end of June, all three sites were secure.

Omni Corp's systematic campaign had been stopped.

But the victory came at a cost.

The Glastonbury Heartstone had cracked. Not destroyed, but damaged. Its power reduced, its threads weakened. It would survive, but it would never be as strong as before.

Penelope returned to Asterly knowing they'd won the battle but understanding the true price of victory. Every use of the Sight at scale, every dramatic intervention, every emergency working damaged the very thing they were trying to protect.

"We can't keep doing this," she said to Rhys as they drove home. "Every time we use the Heartstone's full power, we weaken it. Win enough battles this way, and there won't be anything left to protect."

"So what's the alternative?"

"Prevention. We stop sites from reaching crisis point. Build stronger communities before Omni Corp targets them. Teach people to value connection before it's threatened."

"That's a generational project."

"Then we'd better start now."

CHAPTER SEVENTEEN

Summer deepened into autumn, and the Guardian Network shifted from defensive to proactive strategy.

Penelope established training programs. Young guardians learning from experienced ones. Techniques documented and shared. Resources pooled. What had started as desperate defense was becoming something structured, something sustainable.

But in September, everything changed.

Victoria Crane requested a meeting.

The email arrived on a Tuesday morning, professional and direct. *Ms. Lowell, I believe it's time we spoke face to face. Omni Corp and the Guardian Network have been at war for nearly a year. Perhaps there's a better way forward. I'll be in the Cotswolds next week. Shall we say Thursday, 2 PM, at your convenience?*

Penelope showed the email to Rhys and the other guardians gathered at Sunlit Grove for a quarterly meeting.

"It's a trap," David said immediately.

"Maybe. Or maybe she's serious." Penelope leaned back in her chair. "We've cost them millions. Three major sites defended, countless smaller victories. Maybe they're ready to negotiate."

"Or maybe they're trying to find our weak point," Rhian countered.

"Either way, I think we need to hear what she has to say."

The meeting on Thursday took place at a neutral location. A hotel in Cheltenham, expensive and anonymous. Victoria Crane arrived alone, which surprised Penelope. No lawyers, no assistants, just the Chief Acquisition Officer herself.

They met in a private conference room. Crane was in her fifties, expensively dressed, with the kind of polished competence that reminded Penelope of her old corporate self.

"Ms. Lowell. Thank you for agreeing to meet." Crane sat, gestured for Penelope to do the same. "I'll be direct. The Guardian Network has proven more effective than we anticipated. You've organized what we thought were isolated holdouts into an actual resistance. It's... impressive."

"Is this where you offer to buy me off?"

"No. This is where I propose a truce."

Penelope blinked, surprised. "A truce."

"Omni Corp is a business. We develop properties. We make money. But we're not ideologically opposed to community or connection. We're just pragmatic about what can be preserved and what can't." Crane pulled out a document. "What if we could agree on boundaries? You maintain your seventeen sites. We cease active operations against them. In exchange, you don't interfere with our developments elsewhere."

"You want us to let you destroy other Heartstones."

"I want us to stop wasting resources fighting each other. The sites you've defended will survive. The ones you can't defend will be developed. Everyone gets something."

"Except the communities you destroy."

"Ms. Lowell, be realistic. There are hundreds of potential development sites across the UK. You can't save them all. You don't have the resources, the guardians, or the time. Better to preserve what you can than burn out trying to protect everything."

It was logical. Tempting, even. Accept that some sites would be lost. Focus resources on the ones they could definitely save.

"No," Penelope said.

"No?"

"No deal. We're not giving up on sites just because they're hard to defend. We're not accepting that some communities deserve connection and others don't. We'll keep fighting. All of us. For every site."

Crane's expression hardened. "Then you'll lose. Maybe not today. Maybe not this year. But eventually, you'll burn out. Your Heartstones will crack from overuse. Your guardians will exhaust themselves. And we'll still be here, patient and well-funded, waiting for you to collapse."

"Then we'll collapse fighting."

"That's remarkably stupid."

"Maybe. But it's what guardians do."

Penelope stood and walked out.

Rhys was waiting in the lobby. "How did it go?"

"She offered a truce. Preserve our current sites in exchange for letting them develop everywhere else."

"And you said?"

"No."

He smiled, fierce and proud. "That's my Seer."

But that night, alone in Eleanor's study, Penelope wondered if she'd made the right choice. Crane was correct. They couldn't save every site. Didn't have the resources. Would eventually burn out.

Maybe accepting partial victory was smarter than fighting for impossible perfection.

"You're doubting yourself," Rhys said from the doorway.

"Crane was right. We can't save everyone."

"No. But we can try. That's the difference between us and them. They see communities as resources to be managed. We see them as worth fighting for, even when the fight seems impossible."

"That's naive."

"That's human." He moved into the room, sat beside her. "Eleanor fought alone for ten years. Knew she was losing, knew the threads were weakening, kept fighting anyway. Because the alternative was giving up. Accepting that connection doesn't matter. She couldn't do that. And neither can you."

Penelope leaned against him, feeling the dawn-gold thread pulse with warmth. He was right. The fight might be impossible. But it was their fight. And they'd keep fighting until they couldn't anymore.

CHAPTER EIGHTEEN

Winter brought new threats.

January arrived with frost and fury, and with it, a coordinated assault from Omni Corp that made their previous efforts look tentative.

Twenty sites under attack simultaneously.

The calls started coming in the first week of the new year. Guardians from across the UK reaching out through the network Penelope and Rhys had spent months building. Compulsory purchase orders filed. Development proposals submitted. Legal pressure mounting at sites from Cornwall to Scotland.

It was systematic. Overwhelming. Designed to fragment the Guardian Network's response, force them to choose which sites to defend and which to abandon.

Penelope stood in Eleanor's study, looking at the map on the wall. Twenty red pins marking sites under immediate threat. And they were only two people.

"We can't be everywhere at once," Rhys said, his voice tight with frustration. He'd been on the phone for three hours, talking to guardians, trying to coordinate responses, feeling the network strain under pressure it wasn't designed to handle.

"Then we need to prioritize." Penelope hated saying it. Hated choosing which communities deserved defense and which would be sacrificed. But they had no choice. "Which sites are most critical? Where can we make the biggest difference?"

They spent the day making terrible decisions. Glastonbury, Stonehaven, and Whitby rose to the top. Large populations, strong Heartstones, significant cultural importance. If they could defend these three, if they could force Omni Corp to retreat at high profile locations, it might slow the assault elsewhere.

But it meant leaving seventeen other sites to fight alone.

"I hate this," Penelope said, staring at the map. At the sites they were choosing to abandon. Small villages, isolated guardians, communities that would likely fall without support.

"I know. But we're building something sustainable, not throwing ourselves into every battle and burning out." Rhys moved to stand behind her, his hands on her shoulders. "Eleanor tried to save everything alone. It killed her. We have to be smarter."

"Smarter means letting people lose their homes."

"Smarter means surviving long enough to build a network that can actually win. Not just delay the inevitable."

He was right. She knew he was right. But it didn't make the choice hurt less.

They divided the guardian resources. Penelope and Rhys would take Glastonbury, the most legally complex case. Rhian Davies and David Chen would handle Stonehaven, where community organizing would be critical. Moira MacLeod and young Tom Brennan from Dublin would defend Whitby, leveraging the Heartstone's power.

Everyone else would have to manage alone.

The battle for Glastonbury lasted six brutal weeks.

Penelope threw everything she had at it. Legal filings, emergency injunctions, environmental reviews. She used every trick she'd learned in corporate law, every contact she'd maintained, every favor she could call in.

And she used the Sight strategically. Showing key decision makers the threads they were about to sever. Demonstrating what development would cost in terms that mattered, even if they couldn't be measured.

But Omni Corp had learned from past defeats. They brought better lawyers, more sympathetic judges, politicians who owed them favors. They weren't going to lose through legal maneuvering alone.

In February, the compulsory purchase order was approved despite everything Penelope had done.

She sat in a Glastonbury hotel room, the legal notice in her hands, and felt defeat wash over her like ice water.

"We're going to lose," she said to Rhys. "I can feel it. The order is valid. The development will proceed. We've delayed it, but they're going to win."

"Then we use the final option."

She looked at him. "Show everyone. Make the whole town See."

"It could damage the Heartstone permanently. Maybe destroy it."

"And if we don't, Omni Corp will definitely destroy it. At least this way we go down fighting."

They made the calls. To Rhian, to David, to Moira. Explaining the plan, the risks, the potential consequences. Would the other sites follow suit if Glastonbury attempted this desperate working?

The vote was unanimous across all three sites. Do it. Show them. Make the choice so stark that no one could support development afterward.

On the Summer Solstice, when Glastonbury was packed with tourists and residents, when the Heartstone's power was at its peak, they executed the working.

Fifteen guardians linked together. A chain of Seers and sensitives, all channeling power through their respective Heartstones. Penelope, Rhian, and Moira as focal points at the three sites. Their Guardians anchoring them.

For ten minutes, everyone in all three towns could see the threads.

The full majesty of the Tethering Light made visible. Connections spanning generations, bonds that had survived wars and plagues and social change. The accumulated weight of community made manifest.

Tourists wept. Residents stood transfixed. Developers and politicians fell silent as they understood what they'd been about to destroy.

The compulsory purchase orders were withdrawn the next day. All three sites. Simultaneous retreat by Omni Corp in the face of public outcry they hadn't anticipated.

But the victory came at a terrible cost.

The Glastonbury Heartstone cracked. Not destroyed, but damaged. Its power reduced, its threads weakened. Stonehaven and Whitby suffered similar damage. They'd won the battle, but wounded the very things they were trying to protect.

Penelope returned to Asterly in early July, exhausted and heartsick.

"Three sites saved," she told Mrs. Bramble over tea. "But seventeen others fell while we were fighting. Seventeen communities that called for help and got nothing because we were spread too thin."

"You can't save everyone, dear."

"Eleanor would have tried."

"And Eleanor died at sixty eight, worn out from trying. You're building something that will outlast you. That's more important than winning every battle."

That night, Penelope stood in the oak grove, hand on Asterly's Heartstone. It pulsed steady and strong. Undamaged, because she'd been able to defend it properly. But elsewhere, sixteen Heartstones had gone dark. Sixteen communities severed.

Rhys found her there. "We won."

"Did we? How many guardians gave up after their sites fell? How many communities are fractured beyond repair? How many threads were permanently severed while we were saving three places?"

"More than I want to count. But Penelope, we couldn't save them all. We never could. The best we can do is save what we can and build a network strong enough to prevent this from happening again."

"And if that's not enough?"

"Then we keep fighting anyway. Because the alternative is giving up. Accepting that connection doesn't matter. That communities are disposable." He pulled her close. "We're not giving up. We're just learning to fight smarter."

She leaned against him, feeling the dawn gold thread pulse between them. Stronger than ever despite the strain of the last six months. Or maybe because of it.

"I love you," she said.

"I love you too. And we're going to win this war. Not every battle. But the war."

CHAPTER NINETEEN

The call came at 3:17 AM.

Penelope fumbled for her phone in the darkness, Rhys stirring beside her. The number was unfamiliar. British. Somerset area code.

"Hello?"

"Penelope Lowell?" The voice was young, female, shaking with barely controlled panic. "My name is Sarah Chen. I'm in Glastonbury. You don't know me, but my grandmother, her name was Li Chen, she corresponded with Eleanor Lowell back in the nineties, and I found her journals, and there's a blue thread, and I don't know what to do..."

Penelope sat up, fully awake. "Slow down. What's happening?"

"They're here. Right now. Omni Corp, or, no, they're calling themselves 'Heritage Acquisitions' now, but it's the same company. They bought the Chalice Hotel. The one on Wellhouse Lane. The one that sits directly over our Heartstone."

"When?"

"Six months ago. We didn't know. They used shell companies, offshore trusts. The demolition starts at dawn. Six hours from now. They're tearing it down to build luxury flats, and the Heartstone is underneath..."

"It'll be destroyed."

"Yes." Sarah's voice was barely a whisper. "And I'm alone here. My grandmother died in August. She was the guardian for forty-three years, and I've been trying to hold it together, but I don't know what I'm doing. The threads are breaking. Half the town has sold. I can feel the Heartstone weakening..." She choked on a sob. "I sent out a blue thread two months ago. I've been waiting for help. I thought no one could see it."

Penelope's heart clenched. Two months. Sarah had been calling for help for two months.

"I see it," Penelope said. "We're coming. Right now. Give me your address."

"You can't get here in time. Glastonbury is three hours away, and they start at dawn. That's six hours. Even if you left right now..."

"Then we have six hours." Penelope was already out of bed. Rhys was up too, understanding immediately. "Stay by your Heartstone. Keep it stable. We're coming."

They were on the road by 3:30 AM, Rhys driving while Penelope made calls. Emergency injunctions. Historic preservation claims. Anything to buy time.

Every legal avenue led nowhere. The purchase was

legitimate. The permits filed. No grounds to stop it.

At 4:15, Sarah called again. "The threads are breaking faster. The Patel family just accepted a buyout. That's twelve families gone."

"Hold on. We're an hour and a half out."

At 5:30: "The demolition crew just arrived. They're setting up. The Heartstone... I can feel it dimming."

"Thirty minutes away."

At 5:45, Penelope heard it through the phone. Heavy machinery starting. Grinding gears. Hydraulic hiss.

"They're starting early," Sarah whispered. "They're not waiting for dawn."

"Sarah, get away from the building. If the Heartstone fractures..."

"I'm not leaving it. If it dies, it dies with someone who loves it."

Penelope heard the first impact. Steel teeth biting brick. Sarah's sharp intake of breath.

"I can see it cracking. The Heartstone. It's glowing brighter. That's not good, is it?"

"Sarah, get back..."

The line went dead.

They arrived at 6:47 AM. Seventeen minutes after the Heartstone shattered.

The Chalice Hotel was half collapsed, Victorian facade

reduced to rubble. Demolition crew working methodically. Dust hung like fog.

Beneath the rubble, through the broken foundation, Penelope could See the Heartstone remains. Grey stone fragments. No longer glowing. Threads severed, withering, dissolving like spider silk in rain.

Sarah Chen sat on the curb across the street, arms wrapped around her knees, face streaked with dust and tears. Young, maybe twenty-five, short dark hair, grandmother's journals clutched to her chest.

Penelope sat down beside her. Didn't speak. Just sat.

"I called too late," Sarah said finally. "I should have reached out sooner. Grandmother always said connecting with other guardians was dangerous. I believed her. I waited too long."

"It's not your fault."

"Isn't it?" Sarah turned with red-rimmed eyes. "I've been the guardian for six months. And I've lost everything my grandmother protected for four decades. The Heartstone is destroyed. The network is broken. What kind of guardian am I?"

Penelope had no answer. Because if they'd moved faster, if they'd reached out to every isolated guardian sooner...

"You sent a blue thread," Penelope said quietly. "You called for help. That took courage."

"It took desperation." Sarah looked at the journals. "Grandmother was so afraid. Of being discovered. Of being thought mad. She protected the Heartstone alone for forty-three years because she was terrified of reaching out. And I inherited that fear. And now it's gone."

Rhys crouched in front of them. "The other sites in Somerset. Are they connected to Glastonbury?"

"Three of them. Wells, Shepton Mallet, and Street. When Glastonbury shattered, those connections weakened."

"Then we go to them," Penelope said. "Today. Right now. We don't let this happen again."

"How do you stop it?" Sarah gestured at the demolition. "They did everything legally. How do you fight that?"

"You build something stronger than fear. You connect. You coordinate. You make it impossible to pick you off one by one." Penelope stood, offering her hand. "Your grandmother protected Glastonbury for forty-three years alone. That's heroic. But we're not doing it alone anymore. Come with us. Help us save the others."

Sarah stared at her hand. Then took it.

Behind them, the hotel collapsed completely. Centuries of history reduced to rubble in seconds.

Somewhere in the wreckage, the last Heartstone fragments turned to dust.

Three sites fell in January alone.

Despite the Guardian Network, despite coordination and shared resources, Omni Corp's systematic campaign was working. Villages in Devon, Norfolk, and the Scottish

Highlands lost their Heartstones. Communities fractured. Guardians gave up or burned out trying to fight alone.

Each loss was like a physical blow.

Penelope felt them through the network. The moment a Heartstone shattered, the web of connections convulsed. Threads snapping across hundreds of miles, the pain of severance rippling through every connected site.

She was in Eleanor's study when the Norfolk Heartstone fell, and the shock of it drove her to her knees.

Rhys was there immediately, his hands on her shoulders, the dawn gold thread anchoring her before she could get lost in the cascade of breaking bonds.

"Come back," he said urgently. "Penelope, come back to yourself."

She gasped, the world swimming back into focus. "Norfolk. It's gone. The guardian, Susan... she couldn't hold it. Too much pressure, too many properties sold, the network collapsed."

"How many does that make?"

"Nineteen. Nineteen sites destroyed since Omni Corp began this campaign." She stood shakily. "We're losing, Rhys. They're picking us off one by one, and we can't stop them."

"Then we change tactics. We've been playing defense. Maybe it's time to attack."

"Attack how? We're guardians, not corporate raiders."

"No, but you're a lawyer. And I've been doing research." He pulled out his laptop, showed her files he'd been compiling. "Omni Corp's financial records. Development proposals. Property acquisitions. I've found irregularities. Possible fraud, environmental violations, political bribes."

Penelope's mind, trained in corporate law, immediately engaged. She scanned the documents, seeing what Rhys had found. Money moving through shell companies. Environmental impact assessments that were clearly fabricated. Planning permissions granted impossibly quickly.

"This is evidence of systematic corruption," she said slowly. "If we can prove it, if we can get this to the right authorities..."

"We can cripple them legally. Make Omni Corp too toxic to touch. Force them to abandon not just one site, but their entire UK operation."

"That's ambitious. And dangerous. If we go after them this way, they'll retaliate. They'll come after us personally, not just the sites."

"Let them. We're not isolated guardians anymore. We're an organized network. Let them try to fight all of us at once."

Over the next two months, Penelope built a legal case that would have made her old corporate partners proud. She compiled evidence, contacted environmental organizations, reached out to investigative journalists. And she used her network of guardian contacts to gather information from every site Omni Corp had ever developed.

The pattern became undeniable. Systematic corruption

spanning decades. Political bribes, fraudulent assessments, environmental damage deliberately concealed. Site after site showing the same playbook.

In March, she handed the complete case file to three organizations simultaneously. The Serious Fraud Office, the Environmental Agency, and a team of investigative journalists at The Guardian.

The response was immediate.

Front page headlines. Parliamentary inquiries. Criminal investigations. Omni Corp's leadership went into damage control, but the evidence was overwhelming.

Within a week, their stock price had dropped forty percent. Within a month, their CEO had resigned. By April, the company was facing criminal charges and environmental lawsuits across multiple jurisdictions.

But corporations didn't die easily.

Omni Corp restructured, brought in crisis management teams, started settlement negotiations. They abandoned active operations at contested sites, but they didn't surrender. Just reorganized under new leadership and new strategies.

"We hurt them," Penelope said, watching the news coverage. "But we didn't stop them."

"We stopped this campaign," Rhys pointed out. "That's something. How many sites were saved because Omni Corp was forced to retreat?"

"Twelve active sites preserved. But nineteen already lost. That's not a victory. That's acceptable losses."

"It's survival. And it bought us time to build something stronger."

He was right. The legal assault had given the Guardian Network breathing room. Sites that had been on the brink now had months or years to strengthen their communities, establish protections, build resistance.

But the cost had been steep.

Penelope had made enemies. Powerful ones. People in Omni Corp's leadership who knew her name now, who saw her not as a minor irritant but as a genuine threat.

In May, she started receiving threats. Anonymous emails. Strange cars parked near Sunlit Grove. Photos of her and Rhys taken from a distance, sent to her phone with no message attached.

"They're trying to intimidate you," Rhys said, looking at the latest photo. "Make you back down."

"It's working. I'm terrified." She paced Eleanor's study, unable to sit still. "What if they don't just target me? What if they go after the village? After you?"

"Then we'll deal with it. Together. Penelope, you can't let fear make you retreat now. Not when we're finally winning."

"Are we winning? Nineteen sites destroyed. Countless communities fractured. Guardians burned out or giving up. How is that winning?"

"Because before you started organizing, every site fought alone and lost alone. Now we fight together. Share resources.

Support each other. That's a foundation for actual resistance, not just delaying the inevitable."

She wanted to believe him. But the fear was real. The threats were real. And the weight of responsibility, the knowledge that her choices affected dozens of sites and hundreds of guardians, was crushing.

That night, she couldn't sleep. She went to the oak grove, sat beside the Heartstone, and opened the Sight fully.

The network spread before her. Gold and silver and bronze threads connecting Asterly to other sites. The Guardian Network made visible. Strongest in the UK, but threads stretching to Ireland, to France, to Germany. Connections forming across Europe as word spread about what they'd built.

It was beautiful. Fragile. Worth protecting.

And it was hers to defend.

Eleanor had protected one Heartstone for forty three years. Penelope was responsible for dozens. The weight of it should have been paralyzing.

Instead, looking at the network, seeing how connections bred more connections, how strength in one place strengthened others, she felt something else.

Hope.

They were building something that could survive her. That could grow beyond anything Eleanor had imagined. A true network of resistance that wasn't dependent on individual heroes but on collective strength.

Rhys found her there at dawn. "You've been out here all

night."

"I've been thinking. About what we're building. About what comes next."

"And?"

"And we can't just defend anymore. We need to prevent sites from reaching crisis in the first place. Teach communities to value connection before it's threatened. Build cultural understanding of what the threads mean." She stood, brushing frost from her clothes. "We need to go public. Not with magic, but with the concept. Connection matters. Community matters. There are things worth protecting that can't be quantified."

"That's a generational project."

"Then we'd better start now."

CHAPTER TWENTY

The shift from defense to education happened gradually, then all at once.

In June, Penelope published an article in The Guardian. Not about magic or Heartstones, but about community resilience. About how certain villages resisted development pressure not through legal tricks but through strong social bonds. About the value of connection in an increasingly disconnected world.

The response was overwhelming.

Requests for interviews, speaking engagements, consulting work. Urban planners wanted to understand how to build stronger communities. Local governments asked for guidance on preserving village identity. Academics reached out to study the phenomenon.

Penelope became, unexpectedly, a public figure.

"This is strange," she told Rhys after her third television interview. "I'm explaining the Tethering Light without mentioning threads or magic. Just talking about connection and community in normal language. And people are listening. "

"Because you're telling the truth. Just in words they can accept."

The Guardian Network formalized that summer. No longer just an informal collection of isolated guardians, they registered as an official NGO: The Heritage Connection Network. On paper, they were about preserving cultural heritage and community bonds. In reality, they were protecting Heartstones.

But the public facing work was real too. They developed training programs for communities facing development pressure. Published research on social resilience. Consulted with governments on how to support rural communities without destroying what made them valuable.

And quietly, beneath the public work, they continued protecting sites. Smarter now. More strategic. Choosing battles they could win, building long term resistance, creating legal and cultural frameworks that would survive beyond individual guardians.

In September, Penelope received an unexpected letter.

It was from Victoria Crane, Omni Corp's former Chief Acquisition Officer. The woman who'd shown her the map of destroyed sites, who'd offered a truce Penelope had refused.

Ms. Lowell,

I hope this finds you well. I've been following your work with interest. The Heritage Connection Network is impressive. More impressive is that you've managed to mainstreamed resistance to corporate development without anyone realizing how threatening it actually is to people like my former employers.

I'm writing because I'd like to meet. Not as enemies. As someone who understands what you're doing and wants to help.

I left Omni Corp in April, after the scandal you orchestrated. I've spent the months since reevaluating many things. About connection. About community. About what actually matters.

I'd like to discuss joining your efforts. I have knowledge of how companies like Omni Corp operate. Strategies they use. Weaknesses they hide. That information could be valuable to you.

No obligation. Just coffee and conversation.

Victoria Crane

Penelope showed the letter to Rhys and the other senior guardians during their monthly meeting.

"It's a trap," David Chen said immediately.

"Maybe," Penelope agreed. "Or maybe she's genuine. People can change. Can realize they were wrong."

"After systematically destroying seventeen Heartstone sites? I doubt her conscience suddenly woke up."

"But if she's serious," Moira pointed out, "if she genuinely wants to help, the intelligence she could provide would be invaluable. We'd know exactly how to defend against corporate strategies we've only been guessing at."

The network voted. Narrow approval to meet with Crane, but with precautions. Public location. Multiple guardians present. No sensitive information shared until her motivations were proven.

They met in a London café in October. Penelope and Rhys on one side, Victoria Crane on the other.

She looked different from the polished executive Penelope remembered. Older, tired, less certain.

"Thank you for coming," Crane began. "I wasn't sure you would."

"We're here. Talk."

Crane pulled out a folder. "Everything I know about Omni Corp's replacement strategy. They've restructured, rebranded, learned from their mistakes. They're not calling themselves Omni Corp anymore. They're operating through dozens of subsidiary companies, harder to track, harder to target legally. But their goal is the same. Acquire and develop sites with strong community identity."

She spread documents across the table. Corporate structures, development plans, target lists.

"This site here," she pointed to one document. "Kirkwall in Orkney. They're planning to approach property owners starting next month. And this one. Hay on Wye. Initial acquisitions already underway."

Penelope studied the documents. They were genuine. Current intelligence that would let the Guardian Network get ahead of threats for the first time instead of constantly reacting.

"Why are you helping us?" she asked.

Crane was quiet for a moment. Then, "Because I spent twenty years destroying communities and telling myself it was just business. And then you showed me what I was actually doing. Not in that first meeting. But later, when I saw the villages we'd developed. Really looked at them. Saw what we'd turned them into."

"Ghost towns for tourists."

"Worse. Corpses of communities pretending to be alive. People living in isolation surrounded by neighbors they don't know. That's not just business. That's systematic destruction of something essential. And I was good at it."

She met Penelope's eyes. "I can't undo what I've done. But I can help you prevent it from happening elsewhere. If you'll let me."

Through the dawn gold thread, Penelope felt Rhys's uncertainty mirroring her own. This could be manipulation. Crane could be feeding them false information, setting a trap.

Or she could be genuine. A convert who understood the cost of severance because she'd caused it.

"We'll take your intelligence," Penelope decided. "And we'll verify it independently before acting. If it's good, if it helps us protect sites, we can discuss deeper cooperation. But Victoria? If you're lying, if this is some elaborate strategy to infiltrate the network, you'll regret it."

"I understand. And I am not lying."

Over the next three months, Crane's intelligence proved

accurate. The Guardian Network stopped development attempts at Kirkwall and Hay on Wye before they gained momentum. Protected two sites that would have been lost without advance warning.

Slowly, cautiously, they brought Crane deeper into the network. Never showing her the magical elements, but letting her help with strategy, legal defense, corporate intelligence.

She was brilliant at it. Twenty years fighting for developers had taught her exactly how they thought, how they operated, where they were vulnerable.

"You've built something remarkable," she told Penelope after a strategic planning session. "A resistance network masquerading as a heritage organization. It's... elegant."

"It's necessary. People like your former employers don't stop just because we ask nicely."

"No. They stop because resistance becomes more expensive than the potential profit. You've made yourselves expensive. That's smart."

By the end of the year, the Guardian Network had stabilized. Forty two active sites protected across the UK and Ireland. Training programs running in twenty communities. Legal frameworks established. Public support growing.

They weren't just surviving anymore. They were winning.

Slowly. One community at a time. But winning.

And for the first time since Penelope had inherited Sunlit Grove, she allowed herself to hope that this could actually work. That connection could be protected. That community could survive in a world designed to destroy it.

Eleanor had fought alone and died exhausted.

Penelope was fighting with an army. And they were just getting started.

CHAPTER TWENTY-ONE

Spring arrived with unexpected news.

Omni Corp, restructured and rebranded as "Community Futures Ltd," was collapsing under the weight of its own corruption. The criminal investigations Penelope had triggered were yielding prosecutions. Environmental lawsuits were draining resources. Political allies were distancing themselves.

In March, the company declared bankruptcy.

The Guardian Network celebrated cautiously. Victory felt real but incomplete. Other developers would rise. The forces that profited from severance wouldn't disappear just because one company fell.

But it was still victory.

"Forty seven sites across the UK and Ireland," Penelope told the network during their spring conference. Eighty guardians gathered at Sunlit Grove, the house Eleanor had protected alone now hosting an international gathering. "All stable. All strengthening. We've built something that's surviving."

"More than surviving," Rhian Davies added. "We're growing. Guardians in France have reached out. Germany. Spain. The network is going global."

It was true. Word had spread. Other countries had Heartstones, had guardians fighting isolated battles. The model Penelope and Rhys had built was replicating across Europe.

"We need to formalize the international connection," Moira MacLeod said. "Create actual structure for cross border cooperation. European developers operate globally. Our resistance needs to as well."

They spent two days planning. By the end, they'd established the International Heritage Connection Network. Formal organization with representatives from twelve countries. Shared resources, coordinated strategy, genuine solidarity.

Eleanor's dream of connected guardians had become real.

But success brought new challenges.

In May, Penelope discovered she was pregnant.

She told Rhys in the oak grove, beside the Heartstone that had brought them together. "I'm going to have a baby."

His face transformed. Joy, fear, wonder all at once. "Are you... how do you feel?"

"Terrified. Thrilled. Completely unprepared." She laughed shakily. "I've been so focused on protecting Heartstones, I never thought about protecting a child."

"We'll figure it out. Together."

"What if the baby has the Sight? What if she's a Seer like Eleanor and me? That's a heavy burden to inherit."

"Then we'll teach her. Guide her. Make sure she's not alone the way Eleanor was." He pulled her close. "She'll have both parents. She'll have the entire Guardian Network. She'll never fight alone."

They married quietly in June. A small ceremony in Asterly with the village attending. Mrs. Bramble cried. Maeve made the cake. And the Heartstone pulsed contentedly as Penelope and Rhys made promises that went deeper than words, bound by the dawn gold thread that had become unbreakable.

The pregnancy transformed Penelope's perspective on the work.

"I can't keep traveling constantly," she told the network in July. "I need to stay closer to home for the next few months."

"Then we'll adapt," David said simply. "The network was never dependent on you being everywhere. We've grown beyond that."

It was true. What had started with Penelope and Rhys desperately trying to save sites one at a time had become something self sustaining. Regional coordinators, trained guardians, established protocols. The network functioned whether or not its founders were constantly firefighting.

"This is what we wanted," Rhys reminded her. "Something that could outlast us. Something sustainable."

In September, they hosted a gathering of young guardians.

Seers and Guardians in training, ranging from teenagers to people in their thirties. The next generation who would carry the work forward.

Watching them learn, seeing their dedication, Penelope understood something fundamental. The fight wouldn't end in her lifetime. Or her daughter's. Connection would always need defending. But they'd built tools for that defense that could be passed down.

Her daughter was born in December. Ella Rose, six pounds and perfect. And when Penelope held her for the first time, opened the Sight just slightly, she saw it.

A faint golden thread connecting Ella to the Heartstone. Dormant, like Penelope's had been. But there.

Her daughter was a Seer.

The burden Eleanor had carried, that Penelope now carried, would pass to Ella someday.

But unlike Eleanor, unlike Penelope, Ella would never fight alone. She'd have parents who understood. A network ready to support her. A world that, slowly, was learning to value connection again.

"She's going to be amazing," Rhys whispered, looking at their daughter.

"She's going to be safe," Penelope corrected. "That's all I want. For her to grow up in a world where protecting connection isn't so hard. Where communities aren't constantly under siege."

"Then we'd better keep building that world."

CHAPTER TWENTY-TWO

Ella's first year passed in a blur of sleepless nights and quiet joy.

Penelope scaled back her network responsibilities, focusing on local work. Asterly thrived under her lighter touch. The village had learned to maintain itself, to value connections without constant Seer intervention.

That was the real victory. Not dramatic saves, but sustainable community.

In Ella's second spring, new threats emerged. Not from developers, but from technology.

Social media companies were discovering that isolation was profitable. Algorithms designed to keep people engaged were inadvertently severing real world connections. People spent hours on devices, neglecting face to face relationships. The threads were fraying in new ways.

"This is harder to fight," Penelope told a network meeting. "Developers we could battle legally. But how do you fight technology that people willingly embrace?"

"Education," Victoria Crane suggested. She'd become an invaluable network member, her corporate knowledge helping them stay ahead of threats. "Show people what they're losing. Make the cost of digital isolation visible."

They tried. Published research on social fragmentation. Ran programs teaching digital wellness. Advocated for technology that supported connection rather than replacing it.

It was slow work. Frustrating. But gradually, cultural conversation shifted. People started questioning whether constant connectivity was actually connecting them.

When Ella turned three, Penelope took her to the Heartstone for the first time.

"What is it, Mama?" Ella asked, staring at the glowing stone.

"It's the heart of our village. The thing that keeps everyone connected."

"I can see lines. Pretty gold lines."

Penelope's breath caught. Ella was too young for the Sight to manifest fully. But she could see something. Sense the threads.

"Yes, sweetheart. Those are connections. They're what make people care about each other."

"Like how you and Papa care about me?"

"Exactly like that."

That night, Penelope updated Eleanor's journals. Added her own experiences to the accumulated knowledge. Someday Ella would read these. Would learn about the Tethering Light not from necessity but from legacy.

By Ella's fourth birthday, the Guardian Network had grown to include representatives from twenty three countries. The Tethering Light, they discovered, was truly global. Every culture had versions of it. Different names, different traditions, but the same fundamental network of connection.

"We're not creating something new," Penelope realized. "We're rediscovering something ancient. Something humans understood before we built systems designed to isolate us."

The work evolved. Less about fighting developers, more about cultural preservation. Teaching communities to value connection. Supporting traditional practices that maintained bonds. Resisting the tide of isolation in all its forms.

It wasn't dramatic. But it was working.

Five years after Ella's birth, Penelope stood in Eleanor's study, now truly her own, and looked at what they'd built. Ninety three active Heartstone sites protected globally. Hundreds of communities learning to value connection. A network of guardians supporting each other across continents.

Eleanor had protected one site for forty three years and died exhausted.

Penelope had helped protect hundreds and was thriving.

The difference was community. Partnership. Refusing to fight alone.

"What are you thinking?" Rhys asked from the doorway. Ella was asleep upstairs, worn out from a day playing in the village.

"I'm thinking Eleanor would be proud. And surprised. She thought protecting even one Heartstone was the best anyone could do. We've protected dozens. Built a network she only dreamed about."

"Because you didn't try to do it alone. That was her mistake. She thought she had to carry everything herself."

"And I learned from it. Delegated. Built systems. Let other people help." Penelope moved to the window, looking out at the oak grove. "I'm thinking about stepping back more. Letting the next generation lead."

"You're not even forty."

"I know. But the network doesn't need me the way it once did. Regional coordinators can handle most crises. And I want to be present for Ella. Really present. Not constantly traveling, fighting fires, saving sites."

"What would you do instead?"

"Teach. Write. Document everything we've learned so it's not lost. Train young guardians. Be a resource instead of a leader."

Rhys smiled. "Eleanor spent her whole life fighting. You're building something that doesn't require constant fighting. That's a bigger legacy."

The transition happened gradually over the next year. Penelope remained involved but stepped back from day to day leadership. Younger guardians, trained in the systems she'd built, took over coordination.

And she discovered something unexpected. Stepping back didn't mean abandoning the work. It meant trusting others to carry it. Believing in the network she'd helped create.

Ella turned six. Started school in Asterly's primary school. Made friends. Saw threads connecting them and understood it as naturally as sight or hearing.

"How do other people not see them?" she asked Penelope one day.

"Most people can't. It's a gift our family has."

"It's nice. I like seeing how people are connected. It makes me feel safe."

That's what it came down to. Safety in connection. Knowing you weren't alone. That you were part of something larger than yourself.

That's what the Heartstone protected. What Eleanor had died protecting. What Penelope had learned to protect better.

Not through heroic isolation, but through community.

The lesson had taken too long to learn. But it was learned now. And it would be passed down.

To Ella. To the next generation. To everyone who understood that connection mattered more than profit, more than efficiency, more than any individual achievement.

The Tethering Light would endure.

Because they'd learned to protect it together.

CHAPTER TWENTY-THREE

Ella was seven when she consciously mended her first thread.

A fight between two classmates. Nothing serious, just the kind of petty disagreement that children have. But Penelope, watching from the school gates, saw the thread between them fray.

And she saw Ella, concentrating hard, reach out without touching and weave the frayed ends back together.

That evening, they sat in Eleanor's study. Three generations of journals now. Eleanor's, Penelope's, and the beginnings of what would be Ella's.

"How did you know to do that?" Penelope asked gently.

"It just felt right. Like when you fix a torn page in a book. You want it to be whole again." Ella looked up with those grey green eyes, so like Eleanor's. "Did I do wrong?"

"No, sweetheart. You did exactly right. But it's important to understand what you're doing. You're seeing something most people can't. And with that comes responsibility."

They talked for hours. About the Sight, about guardians, about the weight and wonder of perceiving connections. And Penelope realized she was having a conversation Eleanor never got to have. Teaching her daughter about magic in safety, with support, with love.

No burden placed too early. No isolation. Just gentle guidance toward understanding a gift.

"Will I have to protect the Heartstone someday?" Ella asked.

"Maybe. If you choose to. But that's years away. And if you do, you'll have help. You'll never do it alone."

"Because we're connected. I can see our thread, Mama. It's really bright."

"I know, darling. I see it too."

The Guardian Network, now in its fifteenth year, had evolved beyond anything Penelope had imagined. What had started as desperate defense had become cultural movement.

Schools taught about community connection. Urban planners consulted the network on building socially cohesive developments. Governments passed laws protecting community heritage.

The language shifted. People talked about social capital, community resilience, the value of belonging. Not knowing they were talking about the Tethering Light made visible in policy and practice.

"We're mainstreaming magic," Rhys observed during a network conference in Ella's eighth year. "Making the invisible visible without anyone realizing it's happening."

"That's the only way it could work," Penelope replied. "People won't believe in threads. But they'll believe in community. In connection. In the measurable benefits of strong social bonds."

Asterly had become a model. Researchers studied it. Journalists wrote about it. It was cited in urban planning journals as an example of resilient community design.

No one mentioned the Heartstone. But everyone saw its effects.

Penelope was forty two when she finally finished Eleanor's unfinished work. Every legal protection her great aunt had begun, now completed and strengthened. Asterly was wrapped in so many layers of heritage designation, conservation status, and community ownership that development was functionally impossible.

"Eleanor started this process in 1995," she told Mrs. Bramble over tea. "It's taken me seventeen years to finish what she began."

"But you did finish it. That's what matters."

"I wish she could see it. See what we've built. What her sacrifice made possible."

"She can see it, dear. Through you. Through Ella. Through this village that's thriving because she protected it long enough for you to learn how to make protection sustainable."

That year, the International Heritage Connection Network officially registered as a UN recognized NGO. Global reach. Formal diplomatic standing. Ability to influence policy at the highest levels.

The fight for connection had gone from isolated guardians to international movement.

Ella turned ten. Her Sight strengthened daily. She could see threads across the entire village now. Could sense when connections frayed. Was learning, slowly and safely, how to mend small breaks.

"You're better at this than I was at your age," Penelope told her.

"That's because you're teaching me. Grandmama Eleanor had to learn alone. That must have been scary."

"Very scary. But she did it anyway. Because protecting connection mattered more than being scared."

"Is that what bravery is? Doing scary things because they matter?"

"Exactly that."

Penelope continued teaching. Not just Ella, but young guardians from across the network. Week long intensives at Sunlit Grove where the next generation learned history, technique, strategy.

Many of them would never be Seers. But they could be Guardians, sensitives, community organizers. Could protect the Tethering Light in dozens of ways that didn't require magic.

"The network is self perpetuating now," David Chen observed during one training session. "It'll survive all of us."

"That's the goal. Eleanor's mistake was thinking it all depended on her. We've built something bigger than any individual."

Rhys, now fifty, had scaled back bookshop work to focus full time on the network. His sensitivity had deepened over the years. He still couldn't See threads, but he could sense them so accurately that he functioned almost like a Seer.

"We make a good team," Penelope told him on their tenth anniversary.

"Best team ever. We've saved the world. Or at least the parts of it that value connection."

"Saved is a strong word. Protected, maybe. Made slightly more resilient."

"You're being modest. The world is measurably more connected than it was fifteen years ago. Studies show increasing community engagement, stronger social bonds, more resistance to isolation. That's our work."

It was true. The data bore it out. After decades of decline, social connection metrics were improving. Slowly. In pockets. But improving.

The Tethering Light was strengthening.

Not because of dramatic interventions. But because hundreds of communities had learned to value and maintain their connections. Because the Guardian Network had taught them how.

Penelope turned forty five. Ella turned thirteen. The network celebrated its twentieth anniversary.

And Sunlit Grove, empty for so long before Penelope arrived, was now full of life. Ella's friends. Guardian gatherings. Training sessions. Community meetings.

The house Eleanor had protected in isolation was now a hub of connection.

That, more than anything, felt like honoring Eleanor's legacy.

She'd kept the Heartstone alive long enough to pass it to someone who could do what she couldn't. Build a network. Share the burden. Make protection sustainable.

The work would continue. New threats would emerge. The fight for connection would never end.

But they'd built something that could endure.

Together.

CHAPTER TWENTY-FOUR

Five years later, on Ella's eighteenth birthday, she made a choice.

Penelope and Rhys sat with her in Eleanor's study, surrounded by three generations of journals, and asked the question Eleanor had never been asked.

"Do you want this? The responsibility of being a Seer? Of eventually taking over as Asterly's guardian?"

Ella took her time answering. At eighteen, she was thoughtful, brilliant, kind. She'd grown up seeing threads, understanding connection in ways most people never would.

"I've been thinking about it for years," she said finally. "And yes. But not the way Grandmama Eleanor did it. Not sacrificing everything. I want to protect the Heartstone, but I also want to live. Study at university. Travel. Have relationships that aren't just about the work."

"That's exactly right," Penelope said, relief flooding through her. "The work matters. But so does your life. The network is strong enough now that you don't have to carry everything alone."

"I know. You made sure of that." Ella smiled. "I want to study community psychology. Understand why connection matters from a scientific perspective, not just a magical one. Then come back and help the network with that knowledge."

"That sounds perfect."

Over the next four years, while Ella attended Oxford, the Guardian Network continued evolving. Climate change emerged as a new threat to communities. Displacement, resource competition, environmental degradation. All severing connections.

The network adapted. Worked with environmental organizations. Helped communities build resilience not just socially but environmentally. Recognized that protecting connection meant protecting the places people connected to.

"It's all related," Penelope realized. "Social disconnection. Environmental destruction. Economic exploitation. All part of the same pattern of severance. We can't just protect Heartstones. We have to protect entire ecosystems of connection."

The work grew more complex. More challenging. But also more effective.

By the time Ella graduated, the Guardian Network operated in forty seven countries. Protected over two hundred Heartstone sites. Influenced policy at national and international levels.

Ella came home to Asterly at twenty two. Brilliant, educated, ready to contribute. But on her own terms.

"I'll protect the Heartstone," she told Penelope and Rhys. "But I'll also have a life outside of it. That's not selfish. That's sustainable."

"I know, sweetheart. We never wanted you to sacrifice everything the way Eleanor did."

"She didn't have a choice. I do. Because you built a world where guardians aren't isolated and overwhelmed."

Penelope, now fifty, started the process of formally passing primary responsibility for Asterly's Heartstone to Ella. Not immediately. Not completely. But gradually, teaching her everything Eleanor had taught Penelope, everything Penelope had learned beyond Eleanor's knowledge.

"The Sight is a tool," Penelope explained. "But it's not the only tool. Legal protection, community organization, cultural education. All of that matters as much as mending threads."

"I understand. Magic and mundane working together."

"Exactly."

Rhys, now fifty seven, had become an elder statesman of the network. Young guardians sought his advice. His understanding of the Guardian bond was unmatched. He'd anchored dozens of Seers over the years, teaching them the technique he'd perfected with Penelope.

"You should write a manual," Penelope told him. "Everything you know about being a Guardian. It shouldn't be lost."

So he did. Spent a year documenting everything. The manual became required reading for Guardian training.

The knowledge accumulated over generations. Eleanor's research. Thomas's journals. Penelope's innovations. Rhys's techniques. Ella's academic understanding. All preserved, all shared.

The network was building institutional knowledge that would outlast any individual.

When Penelope turned fifty five, she stepped back from active leadership entirely. Became an advisor, a teacher, a resource. Let the generation she'd trained take over.

It was harder than she'd expected. Letting go. Trusting others to make decisions. Accepting that the network would evolve beyond what she'd intended.

But it was also freeing.

"I've spent twenty five years fighting," she told Rhys. "Maybe it's time to rest."

"You've earned it."

They traveled. Visited Heartstone sites they'd helped protect. Saw communities thriving. Met guardians they'd trained who were doing brilliant work.

In Norway, they found a Heartstone site that had been destroyed a century ago, now being restored by a community that had rediscovered the Tethering Light through the network's research.

"We're not just protecting existing sites," Penelope realized. "We're helping people rebuild what was lost."

"That's more powerful than preservation. That's resurrection."

The global network continued growing. Asia, Africa, South America. Every continent had guardians now, protecting connection in ways appropriate to their cultures.

The Tethering Light was truly universal.

Ella, at twenty five, was doing remarkable work. Combining academic research with magical practice in ways no previous Seer had attempted. Publishing papers on social connection that never mentioned threads but described their effects perfectly.

"She's better than I was," Penelope said proudly.

"She had better training. And she's not carrying the weight alone."

Penelope thought about Eleanor. Who'd died at sixty eight, exhausted and isolated. Who'd spent her last years in pain, worn out from protecting one Heartstone alone.

Eleanor had been brilliant. Dedicated. Self sacrificing.

But her legacy wasn't her solo protection of Asterly. It was what she'd enabled by passing the Heartstone to Penelope. By believing someone could do better. Could build the network Eleanor had only dreamed about.

"I'm going to write her story," Penelope decided. "Everything she did. What she sacrificed. What she made possible. People should know."

She spent the next year writing. Not a journal, but a book. Eleanor's biography. The lonely guardian who protected one village for forty three years and changed the world by trusting her successor.

It was published when Penelope was fifty seven. Became required reading in community development programs. Was cited in academic papers. Influenced policy makers.

Eleanor Lowell, who'd died unknown and exhausted, became a symbol. Of dedication, of sacrifice, of what one person could protect through sheer determination.

And more importantly, of why no one should ever have to do it alone.

The book's dedication was simple:

For Eleanor, who fought alone so others wouldn't have to.

Ella read it and cried. "I wish I'd known her."

"She knew you. Through me. Through her journals. She knew you'd come. Knew the line of Seers would continue. That gave her hope in her darkest years."

"Then I'll honor her. By protecting what she protected. But also by living the life she couldn't."

"That's exactly what she'd want."

CHAPTER TWENTY-FIVE

Penelope was sixty when the paradigm shifted completely.

A new generation, raised with the Guardian Network's teachings, started treating connection as essential infrastructure. The way previous generations had treated roads or electricity.

Urban planners designed cities around community hubs. Governments funded connection initiatives. Businesses were evaluated not just on profit but on social impact.

The Tethering Light, never named but always present, had become mainstream.

"We won," Rhys said, watching news coverage of a new international treaty on community preservation.

"We're winning. It's not over."

"Maybe it doesn't have to be a war anymore. Maybe

we've shifted culture enough that protection becomes default instead of constant struggle."

He was right. The work was changing. Less crisis intervention. More proactive cultivation of connection. Teaching communities to maintain their own threads before they frayed.

Ella, now thirty two, had become one of the network's most influential voices. Her research bridged academic and magical understanding. She'd trained a new generation of guardians who saw their role as educators and supporters, not solo protectors.

"I'm doing what you taught me," she told Penelope. "Building systems that don't depend on individuals. Making protection sustainable."

"You're doing it better than I ever did."

Grandchildren arrived. Ella's twins, born when Penelope was sixty three. A boy and a girl. Both showing early signs of Sight sensitivity.

The fourth generation of Seers.

Penelope held them and understood something profound. She'd spent her life protecting connection. But her real legacy wasn't the sites she'd saved. It was the family she'd built. The daughter she'd raised. The grandchildren who'd carry the work forward.

Eleanor had died alone. Penelope would die surrounded by family, by community, by the network she'd helped create.

That was victory.

At sixty five, Penelope retired completely from the Guardian Network. Kept her hand in through occasional consultation. But mostly focused on grandchildren, on writing, on quiet work maintaining Asterly's Heartstone.

The village had been her project for thirty five years. It thrived now. Strong threads. Healthy connections. Young families moving in, attracted by genuine community in an increasingly isolated world.

"You did that," Rhys said. Now seventy two, slowed by age but still sharp.

"We did that. Together."

"Best partnership ever."

The dawn gold thread between them, forty years strong now, was so solid it was visible even without the Sight. Other Seers could see it. Commented on its strength. Used it as an example of perfect Guardian bond.

"We got lucky," Penelope said.

"We got chosen. By the threads. By Eleanor. By whatever force guides the Tethering Light." Rhys pulled her close. "And we chose each other. Every day for forty years."

At seventy, Penelope published her final book. Not about Eleanor this time, but about the network. Its history, its principles, its future.

The book ended with a simple statement:

Connection is not a luxury. It's a necessity. The Tethering Light, by whatever name we know it, is what makes us human.

Protecting it isn't just protecting communities. It's protecting our humanity itself.

Eleanor understood that. She gave her life for it.

We've learned to protect it better. Together. Sustainably. In ways that don't require sacrifice.

The work continues. It will always continue. Because forces of severance will always exist.

But so will forces of connection. And as long as we teach each generation to value bonds, to maintain relationships, to choose community over isolation, the Tethering Light will endure.

Not because of guardians or Seers or magic.

Because humans are meant to be connected. And given the choice, given support, given understanding, we choose connection every time.

The book became the network's foundational text. Translated into forty languages. Taught in schools. Referenced in policy documents.

Penelope Lowell, who'd arrived in Asterly thirty nine years ago as a cynical London lawyer, had become one of the most influential community theorists of her generation.

And she'd done it all while never mentioning magic.

At seventy five, slowed by age but still sharp minded, Penelope sat in Eleanor's study, now truly a family archive. Four generations of journals. Eleanor's research. Thomas's wisdom. Her own innovations. Ella's academic insights. The twins' first faltering attempts at documenting what they were learning.

The knowledge was preserved. Would continue. Would grow.

Ella, now forty seven, was the network's primary leader. Brilliant at it. More effective than Penelope had ever been because she'd learned from both successes and mistakes.

The twins, fifteen now, were training properly. Learning gradually. With support. With love. Never alone.

"It worked," Penelope told Rhys. Seventy seven now, still her anchor, still her partner. "Everything we tried to build. It worked."

"Better than worked. It's thriving. Three hundred Heartstone sites protected globally. Cultural shift toward valuing connection. Next generation trained and ready. Eleanor's dream fully realized."

"And we're still here to see it."

Unlike Eleanor, who'd died at sixty eight, exhausted and alone. Penelope was seventy five and thriving. Because she'd never fought alone. Had built partnership, community, sustainability into everything.

That night, standing in the oak grove with Rhys, hand on the Heartstone she'd protected for four decades, Penelope opened the Sight fully.

The network spread before her. Not just Asterly's threads, but connections spanning continents. Gold and silver and bronze and crimson. Three hundred Heartstones pulsing in rhythm. Millions of threads connecting communities.

The Tethering Light, stronger than it had been in centuries.

Because guardians had learned to work together.

"Thank you," Penelope whispered. To Eleanor. To the Heartstone. To the force that had chosen her for this work. "For giving me this. For trusting me with it. For letting me do better than you could alone."

The Heartstone pulsed warm. Approving. Grateful.

And Penelope understood. Eleanor had known. Had chosen her not just because of bloodline, but because she'd believed Penelope could build what Eleanor couldn't. Could finish what Eleanor started.

And Penelope had. Had taken Eleanor's lonely sacrifice and transformed it into global movement. Had turned isolation into community. Had made protection sustainable.

Eleanor's legacy was complete.

And it would continue. Through Ella. Through the twins. Through every guardian trained in the network's methods. Through every community that learned to value connection.

The Tethering Light would endure.

Not because of magic.

Because humans chose connection. Over and over. In small daily acts of kindness and care. In resistance to forces of severance. In communities that valued belonging over profit.

That's what Eleanor had died protecting.

That's what Penelope had lived protecting.

And that's what Ella and her generation would continue protecting.

One thread at a time.

Forever.

CHAPTER TWENTY-SIX

Five years later. Penelope was eighty. Rhys was eighty two. Sunlit Grove hosted the fiftieth anniversary of the Guardian Network.

One hundred and forty seven guardians from thirty two countries filled the house and grounds. The manor Eleanor had protected in solitude, now overflowing with the community she'd made possible.

Penelope, moving slowly now but still sharp, welcomed them from the front steps.

"Eleanor would be overwhelmed," she began. Her voice was softer than it once was, but still carried authority. "She spent forty three years protecting one Heartstone in isolation. And here we are, fifty years after she died, protecting three hundred and sixty two sites globally."

Applause.

"But she'd also be proud. Because we did what she couldn't. We connected. We built a network where guardians support guardians. Where no one fights alone. Where the burden is shared."

More applause.

"The Tethering Light endures not because of individual heroism, but because of collective commitment. Because we taught communities to value connection. Because we made protection sustainable."

She paused, looking out at the gathered guardians. So many faces. So much dedication. So much hope.

"The work continues. New threats emerge constantly. Climate displacement. Digital isolation. Political polarization. All forces of severance that require our attention."

"But we're ready. You're ready. The next generation is ready."

"Because we learned Eleanor's lesson. Connection is worth fighting for. But you can't fight for it alone. You build it together. You maintain it together. You protect it together."

"Thank you all. For continuing this work. For choosing connection. For being the resistance against forces that profit from isolation."

"The Tethering Light endures. Because you make it endure."

The celebration lasted three days. Workshops. Strategy sessions. Social gatherings. Stories shared across languages and cultures.

On the final evening, Penelope and Rhys stood in the oak grove. Surrounded by guardians, by family, by the community they'd built.

Ella was there, now fifty two, still brilliant. The twins, now twenty, already doing remarkable work. Ella's youngest, a daughter of five, showing the first signs of Sight sensitivity.

Five generations of Seers now. Eleanor. Penelope. Ella. The twins. The five year old.

The line continued.

"Look at what you built," Rhys murmured.

"What we built. I couldn't have done this without you."

"Best partnership ever."

The dawn gold thread between them, fifty years strong, blazed bright enough for every Seer present to see. The perfect Guardian bond. The standard by which all others were measured.

"I'm tired," Penelope admitted.

"I know. Me too."

"But it's done. The work is secure. The network is strong. We can rest."

"Not quite yet. One more thing."

Rhys pulled out a small box. Inside, two rings. Simple silver bands engraved with spiral patterns. The spiral of connection. The symbol of the Tethering Light.

"We've been married fifty years. I thought we should

make it official in the network's eyes. Bind our partnership formally, the way Eleanor and Thomas never did."

Penelope smiled. After fifty years, the gesture was unnecessary. But also, perfect.

They exchanged rings as the sun set. As the Heartstone pulsed approval. As guardians from around the world witnessed two people who'd spent half a century protecting connection, making their own connection permanent.

"I love you," Penelope said.

"I love you too. Always have. Always will."

That night, back in Eleanor's study, Penelope opened the oldest journal. The one Eleanor had started in 1955.

The first entry read:

Today I became a Seer. The Sight manifested fully during the spring equinox. I can see the threads now. All of them. It's beautiful. Terrifying. Overwhelming.

Thomas says I'll learn to control it. That the sight is a gift, not a curse. I want to believe him.

But I'm so afraid of getting lost in the network. Of losing myself in all that connection.

Penelope turned to the last entry. Written in 1998, weeks before Eleanor died.

I'm dying. I know this. The Sight has burned me out. Protecting the Heartstone alone for ten years was too much.

But I'm not sad. Because Penelope is coming. My great niece. She has the Sight. I can sense it across the distance.

She'll do what I couldn't. Find her Guardian. Build her network. Protect not just one Heartstone but many.

I've given her everything. All my research. All my knowledge. All my hope.

The Tethering Light will endure. Because she won't be alone.

That's enough. That's everything.

Penelope closed the journal, tears streaming down her face.

"Thank you," she whispered. "For trusting me. For believing I could do better. For giving me this gift."

She picked up her own journal. The one she'd been keeping for fifty years. And she wrote her final entry.

Today the Guardian Network celebrated its fiftieth anniversary. Three hundred and sixty two sites protected. Thousands of communities thriving. Millions of threads maintained.

I'm eighty years old. I've spent half my life protecting the Tethering Light. And I've loved every moment.

Eleanor fought alone and died exhausted. I fought with community and thrived.

That's the lesson I hope future generations remember. Connection isn't just what we protect. It's how we protect it.

Together. Always together.

The work continues. Ella and her generation are ready. Better trained than I was. Better supported. Better equipped.

The Tethering Light will endure.

Not because of Seers or Guardians or magic.

Because humans are meant to be connected. And given the choice, we choose belonging every time.

Eleanor believed that. I've proven it.

And now I can rest.

The light continues because we fight for it.

Together.

Penelope set down her pen. Closed the journal. And knew her work was done.

Outside, in the oak grove, the Heartstone pulsed. Content. Secure. Protected by a network that spanned the globe.

Ella would continue the work. The twins would support her. The next generation would carry it forward.

The Tethering Light would endure.

Not because of one person's sacrifice.

But because thousands of people chose connection. Every single day. In small acts and large. In personal relationships and global movements. In resistance to forces of severance and cultivation of community.

That was Eleanor's legacy. Not her lonely fight, but what that fight had made possible.

And that was Penelope's legacy. Not the sites she'd saved, but the network she'd built that would keep saving them. Generation after generation. Forever.

Rhys found her in the study hours later. She'd fallen asleep in Eleanor's chair, the journals surrounding her, a peaceful smile on her face.

He covered her with a blanket and sat beside her. The dawn gold thread between them glowed warm.

After fifty years, they'd completed what Eleanor started. Had built something that would outlast them both. Had proven that connection could be protected. Sustainably. Collectively. Joyfully.

The fight wasn't over. Would never be over.

But they'd won the war that mattered.

They'd taught the world to value connection again.

And that, more than any individual victory, was enough.

The Tethering Light endured.

Forever.

AUTHOR'S NOTE

To you, the reader, who stepped into the world of Asterly and saw the light,

This story began with a simple, whimsical question: What if we could see the connections that bind us? Not as metaphors, but as tangible, luminous threads? From that single thought, the village of Asterly, the grumpy bookseller, the pragmatic lawyer, and the magic of Sunlit Grove began to weave themselves into existence.

While the magic is fictional, the heart of this story is deeply real. It's a story about finding where you belong. It's about the courage it takes to embrace a truth that defies logic, to choose a messy, beautiful path over a safe, sterile one, and to fight for the people and places that feel like home. Penelope and Rhys's journey is, in its own way, a heartline, a testament to the idea that our most profound connections are often the ones we never saw coming.

Thank you for trusting me to be your Seer and for allowing me to guide you through this particular tapestry. I hope you close this book feeling a little more magic in the air and a little more attuned to the invisible bonds that light up your own world.

With gratitude,

Carys Llewelyn

ACKNOWLEDGEMENTS

No book is written alone, and even a solitary Seer has a community of Guardians.

My first thanks must go to my own steadfast Rhys, my partner, whose unwavering belief is the golden thread that holds my world together.

To my early readers, who acted as the first Guardians of this story, your keen eyes and generous feedback helped mend frayed plots and strengthen the narrative's heartlines.

To the baristas at my local café, who fueled countless writing sessions with excellent coffee and never questioned the distant look in my eyes as I wandered the lanes of a fictional English village.

To every writer whose work has ever made me feel less alone, you taught me the power of a story to connect souls across time and distance.

A special thank you to **MK Storyworks** for their guidance and belief in bringing the Tethering Light to life.

And finally, to you. A story is a silent, static thing until a reader breathes life into it. Thank you for giving this one a home in your imagination. I am currently hard at work on **Book Two: The Full Novel**, where the journey of the Seer and the Guardian will continue!

A GLIMPSE OF THE NEXT THREAD...

The Tethering Light is an eternal force, and though Penelope and Rhys fought the ultimate corporate enemy to secure the Grove, the battle for Asterly was merely the overture to a far grander war, a war fought not for land or profit, but for the very soul of **Connection** itself.

The **celestial blue thread** that sparked from the Heartstone is a desperate beacon, a lifeline cast from a place far beyond the Grove's wooded borders. It hums with profound, ancient sorrow, a silent cry for help that the Grove, tuned by the Seer and Guardian's combined power, can no longer ignore.

The Celestial Blue Calling

This thread, unlike any local heartline Penelope has ever mended, pulls them toward a truth Rhys's grandfather could only whisper about: the Tethering Light is a **global network**, and the phenomenon they fought in Asterly is mirrored in sacred sites around the world.

Penelope and Rhys must now leave the peace of Sunlit Grove, and the life they just built, to follow the blue thread's trail. Their journey will take them deep into the heart of Europe's oldest mystical sites and across continents, where they will discover the origin of the **Sundering Protocol** and the true identity of the power that wielded Omni Corp like a puppet.

A New, Ancient Enemy

Omni Corp was only a shadow, a commercial front for a much older, deeper entity known only as the **Severance**. The Severance is not motivated by greed but by **spiritual nihilism**, a belief that connection is weakness, and that by severing the luminous bonds between people, places, and life itself, they can impose a sterile, absolute order on the universe.

The Severance seeks to **monopolize Silence** and annihilate the memory of the light. They have long tracked the Guardians and Seers, viewing the bond forged between Rhys and Penelope as the single most dangerous catalyst to their plans: **a connection that cannot be broken by machine or malice.**

The Destiny of the Seer and Guardian

In **THE TETHERING LIGHT: BOOK TWO – The Celestial Blue** (Coming Soon), Penelope and Rhys must:

- **Decode the Celestial Thread:** They must unravel the

history of the blue thread's owner and understand why their pain is powerful enough to reach the Heartstone across impossible distances.

- **Wield Global Power:** Penelope must learn to use her Sight to mend heartlines on a global scale, repairing ruptures caused by the Severance across different cultures and spiritual traditions.

- **Protect the Nexus:** Rhys must act as the anchor and Guardian in foreign, challenging lands, ensuring their golden bond remains intact as the only defense against the Severance's ultimate goal: severing the world's luminous heart.

The battle for Sunlit Grove secured their home. Now, the Guardian and the Seer must fight to save the light of the entire world.

The Celestial Blue thread has appeared, the call to adventure has sounded, and the journey of the Seer and the Guardian is only just beginning. Don't wait to continue the fight for the light: **Pre-orders for the full-length novel,** *The Tethering Light: Book Two – The Celestial Blue,* **are available now! Visit our publisher, MK Storyworks, at** www.mkstoryworks.com **to secure your copy and ensure you don't miss the next chapter in Penelope and Rhys's global defense of the heartlines.**

ABOUT THE PUBLISHER

MK Storyworks is a truly global book publisher, dedicated to the timeless mission of connecting compelling authors with enthusiastic readers across the world.

We pride ourselves on curating a diverse and dynamic list that spans the full spectrum of literary interests. Whether you are looking for an immersive escape into a bestselling fiction novel, seeking wisdom and knowledge from groundbreaking non-fiction titles, perfecting a dish with our acclaimed cookbooks, or introducing the magic of reading to the next generation with our enchanting children's books, MK Storyworks delivers stories that inform, entertain, and inspire.

Our commitment to quality, creativity, and global reach ensures that every book we publish finds its place in the hands and hearts of readers, no matter where they are.

Connect with MK Storyworks

Stay up-to-date with our latest releases, author news, and

behind-the-scenes glimpses by connecting with us online:

Website: www.mkstoryworks.com

Social Media:

- YouTube: @mkstoryworks
- Instagram: @mkstoryworks
- Facebook: @mkstoryworks
- X: @mkstoryworks
- Pinterest: @mkstoryworks
- TikTok: @mkstoryworks